The Gold-Crowned Jesus and Other Writings

The people made farming land out of the earth, and the government functionaries made farming land out of the people. In this way the government functionaries stripped the skin of the people and thwacked their bones as the farmers cultivated and tamed the land. They counted the number of the people and conscripted them just like the farmers gathered their harvest.

CHỌNG YANGYONG (1762–1836)

THE GOLD-CROWNED JESUS AND OTHER WRITINGS

Kim Chi Ha

Edited by Chong Sun Kim and Shelly Killen

Illustrations by George Knowlton

ORBIS BOOKS
Maryknoll, New York 10545

Several of the works included in this volume were first published (in Korean) in *The Collected Works of Kim Chi Ha* by Han Yang Sa, Tokyo

Grateful acknowledgement is extended to Autumn Press for permission to reproduce from *Cry of the People and Other Poems* by Kim Chi Ha. These translations are used in the Preface of the present volume. *Cry of the People and Other Poems* can be obtained from Autumn Press at 7 Littell Road, Brookline, MA 02146

Printed in the United States of America

Library of Congress Cataloging in Publication Data

Kim, Chi-ha 1941–
The gold crowned Jesus and other writings.

Includes bibliographical references.
I. Kim, Chong-sun. II. Killen, Shelly.
III. Title.
PL992.415.C46A25 895.7'8'4'09 77-17522
ISBN 0-88344-161-6

Contents

Preface

Two years before his untimely death in 1960, Nobel Prize winner Albert Camus gave a lecture titled "Create Dangerously." Camus addressed his audience on the role of the artist in a society whose existence was threatened daily by barbarism and the rising power of the totalitarian state. This Algerian Frenchman, who was looked upon by many as a singular voice illuminating the problems of the human conscience, stated: "History's amphitheater has always contained the martyr and the lion. The former relied on eternal consolation and the latter on raw historical meat. But until now, the artist was always on the sidelines. He used to sing purposely, for his own sake, or at best to encourage the martyr and make the lion forget his appetite. But now the artist is in the amphitheater."

The South Korean poet Kim Chi Ha is in the center of the blood-drenched amphitheater described by Camus, and while confronting the lions he brings forth glowing poems that have the power to rekindle our faith in our intrinsic capacity to transcend our present savagery. Kim Chi Ha is a Promethean bringer of spiritual light to a world that has plunged into global violence through an unholy desire for omnipotence. Through his courageous conduct and stirring poems, the young Korean poet lifts us from the darkness of our habitual callousness and indifference to human dignity.

Currently sentenced to life imprisonment by the Park Chung Hee regime, for the crime of following the truth of his conscience, Kim Chi Ha resembles Albert Camus, as a man and artist who refuses to remain aloof from the suffering of his fellow creatures. The poet's awesome faith and sympathy for the Korean people and the yellow soil of his homeland have given him an extraordinary capacity to endure imprisonment and harrowing torture. Like Camus, Kim Chi Ha combines his acute intelligence and knowledge of history with an emotional commitment to preserving life that entails personal risk and a constant attunement to the depths of the human condition. As young men, both writers spent time in tuberculosis sanatoriums, facing the reality of their own illness and the preciousness of existence. Neither Camus nor Kim Chi Ha were spared the death of friends and family through the war, and neither grew bitter from grief, but, instead, transcended loss with an increased compassion for humankind.

Albert Camus was a symbol of courageous resistance to barbarism in the 1940s and 1950s. For the present generation, Kim Chi Ha has become a beacon of light in a society that has gained efficiency in its power to destroy life. The South Korean poet speaks not only for his own country but for all the Third World nations that suffer dictatorial governments, foreign control through corporate interests, and states of ruthless oppression, underlined by hysterical frenzy.

Kim Chi Ha speaks with the voice of the Old Testament prophets when he says: "We need purge the wild beasts that lurk in peoples hearts." Close to the insights of Dostoyevsky in *The Possessed*, the poet stands opposed to blind trust in benevolent gifts, noting that "philanthropy served the oppressor by turning the people into a mob of beggars." The poet insists that the only freedom of any consequence is one that emanates from self-determined government, wrought by individuals who can love others as they love themselves. Kim Chi Ha's *Declaration of Conscience* was smuggled out of the prison in Seoul, where he wrote with clarion fervor:

My beliefs spring from a confident love for the common people. I have opposed the Park regime and ridiculed the "Five Bandits" because they are the criminal gansters looting this country. . . . My confidence in the people has led me to trust their ability to determine their own fate. . . . What is democracy? It is an ideology opposed to silence, a system that respects a free logos and freedom of speech. . . .

The chief priests and Pharisees defuse the people's bitter resentment and moral indignation with sentimental charity. The people are emasculated by mercy. . . . In similar situations of bondage and deprivation, prophetic religions of love arise in the wilderness and shake the emotions of the oppressed and mistreated people. The slumbering masses awaken like a thunderclap; their human and divine qualities suddenly shine forth. This is the mystery of resurrection—this is revolution.[1]

Kim Chi Ha has attested to the love he speaks of with deeds of conscience and has revealed hidden truth through the medium of his poetry, resurrected from the blood and bones of the Korean people.

Arrested in 1970 for his poem *Five Bandits*, satirizing government corruption, Kim Chi Ha was imprisoned for writing *The World of Chang Il Tam*, which deals with a robber who becomes a preacher of liberation. He takes from the rich and gives to the poor. Ending up in jail, he preaches revolution to his fellow robbers. Although the work was not completed, the government accused the poet of being the character Chang Il Tam. When the Park government imposed imprisonment and the death sentence upon Kim Chi Ha, they attested to the truth of Camus's statement: "It is not surprising, therefore, that art should be the enemy marked out by every form of oppression. It is not surprising that artists and intellectuals should have been the first victims of modern tyrannies, whether of the Left or the Right. Tyrants know there is in the work of art an emancipatory force, which is mysterious only to those who do not revere it." Liberty and truth will always draw people out of their isolation, just as slavery imposes a crowd of solitudes. The Korean poems that Kim Chi Ha writes from the abyss of solitary confinement do what Camus said every great work of art does: "makes the human face more admirable and richer, . . . and thousands of concentration camps and barred cells are not enough to hide this staggering testimony of dignity."

Born on February 4, 1941, in Cholla province in South Korea, Kim Chi Ha entered the Department of Esthetics of Seoul National University's College of Liberal Arts and Sciences in 1959. During 1961 and 1962 he wandered about the Korean countryside, then, returning to the university, took part in the 1964 student movement activities opposing government policies. During this time he was imprisoned and tortured. After graduating from the university in 1966, he once again took to the road, working at odd jobs and writing. By 1967 his tuberculosis was chronic, and he spent two years in a sanatorium. Between 1968 and 1970 he worked on movie scripts and theater workshops and published *Five Bandits,* which led to his arrest under the repressive anti-Communist laws. In the spring of 1972, the poet published *Groundless Rumors* in a Catholic magazine, *Creation.* Kim Chi Ha was again arrested and confined to a sanatorium in Masan.

Nobuhiko Matsugi, from the Committee to Save Kim Chi Ha, visited the poet in June of 1972. All the petitions that Matsugi had mailed to Korea were mysteriously lost, and the writer felt that he was under constant surveillance during the whole period of his visit. The Park regime had bred a climate of such terror and paranoia that anyone considered to have made remarks unflattering to the government was subject to shadowing, arrest, or torture.

Confined within the sanatorium while his friends were being horrendously brutalized (ruptured intestines, electroshock, fire torture, hanging upside down, swinging in the air, soapy water pumped into the body, etc.),[2] Kim Chi Ha told Matsugi, "I cannot forgive those who torture, but I must because tomorrow is my confession day." The interviewer was deeply impressed by the poet's sincere Catholicism, and noted his broken front tooth and a long scar on his left cheek. When he took a closer look at Kim Chi Ha, he saw that his face was landscaped with small scars.

A charismatic figure who uses the forms of shaman incantations and rich Korean colloquialisms in his poetry, Kim Chi Ha is the only Asian poet to combine the essence of Christian socialism with his native tradition. As his face bears the marks of his faith and strength of heart, so his poems carry the spirit of rebellion hewn from the tragic past of a war-torn, anguished nation. Korea has a long history of chronic poverty, subjection to foreign powers, and protracted internal and external wars.[3] The poet's province, Cholla, was the site of massacres. Rebellious Cholla is known for the poorness of its soil and the "backwardness" of its people.[4] Kim Chi Ha described his land in the poem, "Yellow Dust Road":

> In small *Whadang*[5] village embraced
> Among the sparse bamboo-bushes,
> Blood surges up in every well, every ten years.
> Born in this barren colony,
> Slain under the bayonets, my Father,
> How could the dew in the bamboo-buds that spring
> Forget, ever forget the crystal brightness of May?
> It was a long and cruel summer,
> When even the children were starving,
> That sultry summer of blatant tyranny
> That knew not of the Heavens
> Or the yellow road, eternally our motherland,
> Our hope.

The poet imbues nature with a spiritual being, characterizing the summer of hunger and tyranny as one that "knew not of the heavens." Blood from the innocent, who have been wantonly slain, returns every ten years, and the poet transforms the cry of sorrow into a lament that keeps memory alive and sustains hope in the yellow soil. In *April Blood*, a poem commemorating the South Korean student revolution of 1960 that brought on the collapse of the Syngman Rhee regime,[6] the poet exhorts:

> Burn the external oppression
> Of silence standing aloft in the darkness.
> Oh, April blood
> Fragrance dispersing brightly even in the darkness;
> Crazed by clear bright life.

Kim Chi Ha frequently uses the image of a fire that purifies, and like the Christian mystics he perceives the light within the darkness. Encountering nature with the eye of his heart, the poet speaks directly to the elements as ciphers for a spiritual being. In the poem *Blue Suit* (blue uniforms were worn by South Korean prisoners) he addresses the heavens:

> Vivid blue sky opening
> Through the dark clouds in nightly dreams . . .
> Could I stand in spilling sunrays a moment,
> Willingly would I die imprisoned in the blue suit;
> Were it real,
> Were it now,
> For ever and ever
> Willingly would I die.

The poet's surrender to death is an expression of his adoration for the sheer marvel of existence and the joy of a moment's freedom in the sun. His capacity to endure travail and arduous ordeals of pain is contingent upon an overwhelming passion for the wonder of life.

Kim Chi Ha has not elected martyrdom; it is the false laws and repressive South Korean regime that make his poetry and spontaneous thoughts a crime. Jailed for the authoring of his narrative poem *Five Bandits*, Kim Chi Ha wrote the following introduction to this satirical work:

I want to write a poem with candid and bold words and without any hesitation. It's been a long time since I was last beaten up for writing with an unruly pen. My body is itching to be beaten; my mouth is eager to speak; and my hands are dying to write. Since my urge to write is beyond my control, I have made up my mind to write a story concerning strange bandits. I am doing this knowing that it will invite serious punitive measures, including physical pain.

The utter intensity of Kim Chi Ha's cry is expressed in the lines:

Speak, speak
With torn body
Every wound
As an open lip
As an open tongue.

Kim Chi Ha transcends fear of punishment by answering the call of his blood to burst forth with the truth of heart and mind. He is inspired in the way that Jeremiah and Isaiah were, and his deep respect for the inner power that fires his pen endows his poetry with a thunderous energy. Kim Chi Ha's tremulous appreciation for the sanctity of life is rendered with utter plainness in this beautiful prayer:

Food is heaven
As we eat
God enters us
Food is heaven

Oh, food
Should be shared and eaten by all.

The poet experiences the mystical body of the deity within the food that people share in common. Modern western or eastern people with full bellies cannot say this simple prayer, nor can they sanctify nourishment with a sense of the holy. In the poem *Hunger* the poet personifies the voice of a starving peasant:

I could devour animals by the hundreds, thousands—hard ones.
I want to eat pork, put away fat ones.
I'll eat you.
I've been driven mad by long starvation.
. . . .
I'll even eat human flesh.
Ah, I'm so unbearably hungry
I could eat money.

For an appreciation of the acute hunger described by Kim Chi Ha, we need some understanding of the history of Korea and the dynamics of a social order that has sustained harrowing living conditions for the majority. The famed unification of Korea (A.D. 676), which took place during the Silla period, was achieved through assistance from China. To keep in China's good graces, the Koreans adapted a policy of *sadae* (serve the larger), which entailed bowing to and placating China at the expense of the native peasantry.[7] A naturally hostile environment gave the Koreans an inadequate food supply, and this dearth was heightened by tributes to China and the sustaining of an extravagant and indulgent ruling class. The rulers bled the peasantry and exacted from them both rigid conformity to heartless laws[8] and service in the military; this led to starvation for many. Peasants could be conscripted at any time for both warfare and the various building projects and monuments that the rulers desired for their own glory.

The hunger and deprivation of dignity suffered by the ancient Korean peasants was a monstrous sacrifice to human greed that sowed the seeds of misery and frustration for generations to come. There are numerous accounts in the ancient Korean chronicles of peasants eating grass or the barks of trees to nourish themselves, and there are even more harrowing stories of children offering their flesh to their parents.[9] When Kim Chi Ha's peasant says, "I'll eat roots, gulp down dirt with flowers, and bright red poison mushrooms," he is speaking with the heritage of a people acquainted with the most extreme form of hunger. This situation of grave impoverishment continued on into modern times. During and after the Korean War, garbage collectors sold refuse to market women, who boiled G.I. garbage infested with cigarette butts and chewing gum, and sold this to the people as "U.N. stew."

The condition of excruciating poverty in Korea, coupled with the rigid social order and *sadae* policies, sustained a state of extreme frustration and rage that found an outlet in the traditional religion of shamanism. Buddhism, Confucianism, and Christianity were all adapted as religions in Korea, but the underlying behavior pattern of the people was shaped by shamanism. Although it is currently fashionable in the West to view shamanism as a poetic and therapeutic mode of healing, in Korea shamanism was clothed in superstition and ignorance. An animistic religion that is based on techniques for attaining ecstasy, shamanism employs incantation, trance-like states, and magic ritual as ways of countering evil, which is always viewed as coming from the external world. Korean shamans alternated between states of hysterical frenzy and obsequious passivity that paralleled the country's foreign policy of *sadae*, which fostered bowing before authority figures and venting rage on those below.[10] Oscillation between extremes of politeness and sudden outbursts of violence are characteristic of the Korean people and can be understood both as a reflection of shamanism and adaptation to subjection from their own rulers and foreign powers. Kim Chi Ha characterizes Korean duplicity in his poem, *The Song of the Cherry Bandit:*

The right eye looks at the sky, while the left looks down at the earth.
Two words are spoken with one mouth and each is listened to by two ears.

. . . .

Praise while cursing, spit while bowing.
Laugh when angry, join together when feeling separate.

Kim Chi Ha evokes the healing aspect of shamanism in his vigorous use of incantation for speaking from the heart, with the pulse of his own blood. The poet intentionally uses Korean local dialects that are rich in flavor and meaning and have been looked down upon by the Korean elite, who imitate the mores and styles of the West. By employing shamanistic forms and local dialect, the poet rekindles native Korean traditions that embody the sentiments and aspirations of the peasantry and social outcasts. In doing this, Kim Chi Ha has restored dignity to the people and reclaimed the important inner values that are quickly dying out with the onslaught of "modernization."

Kim Chi Ha inveighs against fearful silence and submission to power-hungry rulers. He cries out for the need of Koreans to stand on their own two feet with pride and join each other in sharing their common burdens. In his own writing he expresses the archaic yearnings that are characteristic of shamanism, but he tempers the ancient vision with a recognition of the profound import of the common welfare. Korean shamanism extols the power of the individual wish and views the wish of an individual as a spiritual entity that persists after death. The poet writes:

All that is left
is to fall
One last chance
to fall
On that sword
On that sword

like a red, red flower
. . . .
Dying
with my blood
to forever rust
your sword

Shaman themes such as return after death and dismemberment are expressed through the figure of Ando in the poem *Groundless Rumors:*

Wild geese, tell my mother
I will return,
I will return even if I am dead—
Even if my body is torn into one thousand or ten thousand pieces.
I will break out through the walls of this jail,
I'll leap over the fence
Even if I have to sell my soul to the devil.
I will return, mother, whatever happens, I will return.

Ando has committed the crime of attempting to stand up despite his poverty-stricken status, "the crime of wasting time in thinking, the crime of looking up at the sky without a feeling of shame," . . . "the crime of insolently avoiding the national policies for more production, export, and construction without a moment's rest." He therefore has had his head, arms, legs, and sexual organs cut off, so he could not breed more of his "seditious" self. Ando can neither sing nor cry, since he has neither head nor eyes nor voice, but from his trunk a sound called "Kung" is driving the people mad. "Kung" is the ghostly presence that wails the truth through the medium of the poet.

Two Korean words that Kim Chi Ha frequently employs in his poetry are: *han* and *t'onggok*. *Han* means a grudge from the recess of the heart, and *t'onggok* is a lamentation from the depths of the heart. Ando, the timid and obedient failure in life, becomes a human being when, after being exhausted, starved, and sickened, he puts his two feet on the ground and cries, "What a bitch this world is." As soon as the grudge and cry are released, handcuffs are put on Ando and he is dragged to court. The poet pounds out the crimes of Ando:

> Thinking up groundless rumors which would mislead innocent people, the crime of intending to voice the same rumors, the crime of voicing the same, the crime of intending to spread the same, the crime of spreading the same, the crime of disrespecting the fatherland, the crime of disgracing his native language, . . . the crime of agitating the mind of the people, the crime of growing weary of life, the crime of escaping from existing customs, . . . the crime of strong-mindedness, and on top of it the crime of violating the special society manipulating law.

Han and *t'onggok* are sacred impulses that embody Korea's history of repressed suffering and rage. By stifling these cries, the law violates what the ancients called "the Will of Heaven." Kim Chi Ha's thunderous voice bears witness to the sky and Ando cannot be silenced. Always the poet writes of return. "Kung" returns the dismembered Ando to his mother; the poet goes back to where his father died. For the archaic shamanistic mind, the dead return when they have been wrongly slain; hence the impulse to cut up their bodies. For the modern mind, the memory of the evil deed returns in the form of conscience. Lady Macbeth cannot ever wash her hands of blood. By going back to the wrong deed and memories of cruel destruction, Kim Chi Ha releases them into the present. By remembering and consciously bearing grief, the poet lifts the shamanistic urge for vengeance into the realm of an action that frees people for renewal. Kim Chi Ha returns in order to go forward again into life. He writes: "I embrace the naked suffering of tomorrow's earth./ Which I must fight for again, laying down my life." As in nature, death is never ending if life is to begin again.

Central to Kim Chi Ha's poetry is the paradoxical role

played by opposites in the crucible of his life. It is the barren soil of Cholla that fertilizes his spirit. From the " . . . hollow scars left by the whip,/ in the shadow of peasants' hollow eyes, . . ./ In the unopened parched lips, and unopened prisons, . . ." the sea of life begins to flow. Life comes from death and spiritual rebellion from the most profound kind of humility in the face of humankind's common application. In his poem *The Sea*, Kim Chi Ha presents the "small, silent sea of anger./ Brimming; while waves gather./ Candle-light permeates the torn body"; shamanistic animism is linked to the Christian mystery of light incarnated in troubled waters.

The Christ of Kim Chi Ha is a man who comes to life when other men wish him to exist and act on their belief with courage and devout faith. In his play *The Gold-Crowned Jesus*, a leper speaks with Christ, imprisoned in concrete:

LEPER: What can be done to free you, Jesus, make you live again so that you can come to us?

JESUS: My power alone is not enough. People like you must help to liberate me. Those who seek only the comforts, wealth, honor, and power of this world, who wish entry to the kingdom of heaven for themselves only and ignore the poor and less fortunate, cannot give me life again. Neither can those who have never suffered loneliness, who remain silent while injustice is done and so acquiesce to it, who are without courage. It is the same with those without courage who are unwilling to resist such evildoers as dictators and other tyrants who inflict great suffering on the weak and poor. Prayer alone is not enough; it is necessary also to act. Only those, though very poor and suffering like yourself, who are generous in spirit and seek to help the poor and the wretched can give me life again. You have helped give me life again. You removed the gold crown from my head and so freed my lips to speak. People like you will be my liberators.

The Jesus of Kim Chi Ha will live again only when people, through their deeds of resistance to cruelty and injustice, recreate him. This view parallels the vision of Kazantzakis, who wrote: "It is not God who will save us—it is we who will save God, by battling, by creating, and by transmuting matter into spirit. God is never created out of happiness or comfort of glory, but out of shame and hunger and tears."

The leper, a symbol of the social outcast, attempts to remove the Christ figure from concrete. Then a priest, a company president, and a policeman appear on stage, astonished by the fact that the gold crown had been taken by the leper. The policeman snatches it away from the leper. The company president takes it away from the policeman, saying that it was his donation, and the priest takes it from the company president, insisting that it belongs to the church. Christ returns to the inert figure of gold and concrete that powerful people and Pharisees choose him to be.

Kim Chi Ha is close to Dostoyevsky and Tolstoy's Christian eschatology, basing redemption on sin or descent into the shadow world. The poet identifies himself with the debased *sangnom*, a stratum of society viewed as subhuman in Korea, that includes prostitutes, beggars, and lepers. The leper, who is most repellent (the company president holds his nose to avoid smelling him) is the redemptive figure, because he is furthest away from the self that we can easily embrace. Unlike the one-dimensional social realist, Kim Chi Ha confronts the shadow self, whose very darkness and seeming ugliness is the source of light and beauty. When the leper asks, "Who put you in prison?" Christ replies:

> You know them very well. They are like the Pharisees. They locked me in a shrine for their own gain. They pray, using my name in a way that prevents my reaching out to poor people like yourself. In my own name, they nailed me down to the cross again.

Jesus tells the leper:

> You are the *only* one who can do it. And through your deeds, and with the help of your people, I will establish the kingdom of heaven

on earth for all. It is your poverty, your wisdom, your generous spirit, and, even more, your courageous resistance against injustice that makes all this possible.

For Christ to live again, people have no need of shamanistic miracles, but the "courageous intent" to protest injustice. The price of this protest has been imprisonment, maiming, torture, and death for the Korean people, who share Kim Chi Ha's conviction.

Mystical in his inner faith, Kim Chi Ha has presented explicit programs for the rejuvenation of Korea. In the play *Chinogi* ("Subduing Bad Devils"), the peasantry is encouraged to believe in a release from their seemingly hopeless despair. The poet states that it is not their fate to lose all of their grain, but the machinery of the government has impoverished them. He enumerates intelligible reasons for their centuries of miserable exploitation and urges them to form collectives and collectively struggle against usurers, speculators, tenant farming, government agrarian policies, and other feudal practices. The poet proposes farmers' cooperatives where teamwork, profit sharing, and distribution of the land are carried out through democratic procedures. Kim Chi Ha's vision of renewal is similar to that of Cesar Chavez, leader of the California farm workers, and, like Chavez, he draws upon intrinsic human dignity as the base for an "agonized violence of love."

The way to achieve freedom and self-determination is the way of voluntary suffering. Kim Chi Ha's own life has been a *via dolorosa* that he records in his poem *Torture Road*, one of the major documents of our century. From prison the poet embraces all of humankind:

Oh, my friends who are not yet liberated. Those friends whose ruptured intestines were spilled out by torture, . . . and those who are crouching in the darkness, with their eyes glaring and gasping with phlegm-rattling breath. My affectionate friends in the prison—"thieves and robbers." Those soldiers who left the peninsula, wept at the moment of separation and later massacred innocent villagers in Vietnam. I was no other than they. They were no other than I.

When the poet likens himself to others who massacred, he takes the shadow self into his own being and transcends all opposition through the power of love. The poet is a saint who calls himself a comic. In 1972 he wrote: "I'm not a Solzhenitsyn, you know. I'm Kim Chi Ha. Not a tragic figure. A comic, like these bad teeth of mine. I feel happy in any situation. But the chance to write freely, that's what I hope for now. The chance to write freely."

There is Swiftian humor and brilliant irony in his parable-poem, *Five Bandits.* The five bandits are a tycoon, an assemblyman, a government official, a general, and a minister. Bandit Number One is surrealistically imaged as a man wearing a custom-made suit tailored of banknotes, with banknote shoes and gloves. He roasts the cabinet minister and boils the vice minister, and "swallows them together with the banknotes that he has collected from taxes, funds borrowed from foreign countries, and other privileges and benefits."

Bandit Number Two "steps forth with his cronies from the National Assembly" as alley foxes, angry dogs, and monkeys yelling slogans:

Revolution, from old evil to new evil!
Renovation, from illegal profiteering to profiteering illegally!
Modernization, from unfair elections to elections unfair!
Physiocracy, from poor farms to abandoned farms!

The third bandit looks "like a rubber balloon with viperous pointed eyes." "He sits in a wide chair as deep as the sea, before a desk as high as the sky. . . . He acts like an obedient shaggy dog when flattering superiors, but like a snarling hunting dog to subordinates. He puts public funds into his left pocket, and bribes for favors done into his right pocket."

Bandit Number Four is a big gorilla, so tall he reaches almost to the heavens. His breast is adorned with medals, and black pistols cling to his body.

The fifth bandit and his cronies "command the national defense with golf clubs in their left hands, while fondling the tits of their mistresses with their right." They chant: "Let's construct a bridge across the Strait of Korea with the bones of those who have starved to death, so we can worship the god of Japan!"

Kim Chi Ha uses the technique of bold exaggeration and caricature, as it was employed in the ancient Korean chronicles.[11] His bestiary of government officials are themselves shamanistic in their passion for adornment, parading of external emblems, and worship of modern gadgets and weaponry. Like the ancient rulers of Korea they ape the manners of foreign powers, sacrifice the welfare of the nation to their own egoistic pleasures, and tell blatant lies while masked as innocent children and virtuous adherents of law and order.

Reverend Sun Myung Moon, the wealthy Korean industrialist-evangelist, belongs in the world of Kim Chi Ha's Five Bandits. Linked frequently with the Korean Central Intelligence Agency and known to own a munitions industry in South Korea, Reverend Moon preaches Christianity, unity, and universal brotherhood, while inducing his followers to solicit some 36 million dollars a year in funds that are channelled back into his numerous foundations and dubious "charities." Kim Chi Ha describes Sun Myung Moon as one who has "sought an ally in the exploiters"; because Reverend Moon tramples on the weak and the poor, the poet views him as hindering any kind of unification in Korea.

In his numerous million-dollar public appearances, Reverend Moon has utilized the traditional shamanistic devices of chanting, colorful spectacles, dancing girls, and a musical troupe known as the Little Korean Angels. Ironically, Sun

Myung Moon's 1976 appearance in New York City coincided with the United States Congress meeting to allocate funds for "armament modernization" in South Korea, with a proposed budget of $495 million. While Moon preached to his audience on the terrors of communism and Congress arranged military aid to one of the most repressive regimes in the world, eighteen prominent political and religious leaders were standing trial in South Korea for the crime of issuing a declaration that called for Park Chung Hee's resignation and the restoration of democracy.

In his court transcript, Kim Chi Ha suggested that perhaps Sun Myung Moon "is the anti-Christ, come to announce that a better world is coming soon." While the notorious preacher dances to the tune of the Korean government and lives in the lap of luxury, Kim Chi Ha and thousands of Koreans labelled dissidents bear palpable witness to their faith from the darkness of their prison cells.

Kim Chi Ha's narrative poem *Ko Kwan* (Part II of *Groundless Rumors)* graphically depicts the nightmare of Korean "modernization." Ko Kwan (the high Korean official) wears "U.S. jockey shorts, a necktie bought in Paris, Chinese green jade cuff links, Scottish tweed pants, and a crocodile belt from the Congo." Each article of clothing, including his wristwatch, is a symbol of external display, with each item produced from the exploitation of the many for the pleasures of the few. Ko Kwan checks into a hotel that catches fire on Christmas Eve. The narrative is based on an actual account of a hotel, which, according to rumor, was opened by President Park Chung Hee and a former head of the KCIA, Lee Hu Rak. In *Ko Kwan* Kim Chi Ha portrays the grotesque horror of a modern *Inferno.* At the time of the fire, desperate figures run from corner to corner, frantically seeking an exit. "Light bulbs pop; liquor bottles explode; windows crack; iron beams heave; fireballs fly; lights flash." And the poet notes: "A steel reinforced building is in the end no safer than a poor farmer's house of thatch."

No one attempts to put the fire out. Everyone tries to flee from a building that has no emergency staircases, because the fire inspector was bribed. The exit to the roof is blocked to prevent guests from leaving without paying their bills. The hotel fire is a metaphor for Korea aflame with hysteria and the madness of "modernization." In this hellish world, even the fire hydrant is only for show. The ultimate realization of how perverse Korean society has become through the efforts of the Park regime is related in an answer to a request to go down the stairs: "You are as mad as the State of Emergency Decrees. . . . Don't you know that fire burns from the bottom up?"

The poet conveys the essence of a frenzied, disintegrating society in *Ko Kwan*, with a black humor that jolts the reader into a rude awakening:

Men and women, having slept in the same room,
Run separately like strangers from each other:
Men to the east! Women to the west!
Women desperately running to the west turn back and run to the east, knowing that the west quarter is on fire.
. . . .
Among the dying, some Japanese shouted,
"Is this modernization?
"Is the lack of an emergency staircase modernization?
"Eat shit, you fools! Some modernization," and plunged to hell.
A guy barely pulled himself up to the window and shouted:
"Damn it! I have to die without spending a single one of my billions of *won* deposited in a Swiss bank account."
Tear drops fell like chicken shit on his cheek as he dropped back into the fire.

The apocalyptic hell that Kim Chi Ha illustrates in *Ko Kwan* is a reality that he and others like him have countered with what he calls an "agonized violence of love."

I reject the violence of oppression and accept the violence of resistance. I reject dehumanizing violence and accept the violence that restores human dignity. It could justly be called a "violence of love." . . .

Violence and destructiveness obviously bring suffering and hardship. But we must sometimes cause and endure suffering. Never is this more true than when the people are dozing in silent submission, when they cannot be awakened from their torpor. To preach "nonviolence" at such a time leaves them defenseless before their enemies. When the people must be awakened and sent resolutely off to battle, violence is unavoidable. Gandhi and Frantz Fanon agonized over this dilemma. Father Camilo Torres took a rifle and joined the people. He died with them, the weapon never fired. The fallen priest with his rifle epitomized godliness. I do not know if his beliefs and methods were correct or not, but the purity of his love always moves me to tears. He staggered along his road to Golgotha with uncertain tread. He was prepared to commit a sin out of a love for others. He was not afraid to burn in the depths of eternal hell. . . .

I do not anticipate or support a "lucky revolution" achieved by a small number of armed groups committing terrorist acts of violence. That is why I have eschewed the formation of membership in secret organizations and have participated in activities consistent with the democratic process: writing and petitions, rallies, and prayer meetings.

My vision of a revolution is the creation of a unified Korea based on freedom, democracy, self-reliance, and peace. More fundamentally, however, it must enable the Korean people to decide their own fate. I can confidently support such a revolution [*Declaration of Conscience*].

Kim Chi Ha's statement of admiration for Camilo Torres and his honest incertitude about the correctness of his beliefs and methods is a poignant indicator of the poet's vulnerable humanity, which chooses imperfection and truthful doubt to the absolute sureties and platitudes of false messianic figures like Reverend Moon. The poet is close to Camus, who also bore the tensions of doubts and contradictions within himself,[12] as a pain that made him more fully human in his continued search for existential truth.

Moon is like the figure of a demented egotist, the King in Kim Chi Ha's *Adoration of a Six Shooter.* The poet employs the forms of the ancient texts here: "One day in the year of the pig, the King held a banquet. A long snake coiled in the rafters of the hall, then suddenly disappeared. Later the king fell ill, his belly swelling more each day. . . . So the king consulted a shaman living deep in the mountains far away." When the king asks the shaman what to do to heal himself of pregnancy, the sorcerer answers:

> Shut everybody's mouth tightly. . . . I recommend that Your Majesty eat 30 million livers of live humans. Best of all are the livers of Communists, known to be the most bitter. But lately they have all been devoured and are therefore hard to come by.

Moon's crusade against communism in Korea is the mask that conceals his amassing of money and power. Park's fervor against non-existent Communists and living dissidents and Christians is hysterical, shamanistic frenzy that underlies his regime's protection of the business interests of Japanese and American corporations.[13] As the ancient shamans used spells and incantation to dispel the king's opponents, so the modern kings are advised to use troops, air force, palace guards, cannons, tanks, and planes. When the King of the *Six Shooter* poem gives orders that a statue of Jesus be ground into powder by guns, "none of the bullets reached or touched the small statue. . . . Instead, the bullets crisscrossed, killing and crushing the troops, until at last all had perished." Kim Chi Ha concludes this poem with a saying of the wise men: "The use of arms and murderous weapons is not the way to happiness but the first step to self-destruction."

Torture Road is the most autobiographical and interior of

Kim Chi Ha's poems. A mixture of prose, poetry, and incantation, *Torture Road* testifies to the poet's alchemical wedding of Korean shamanism with Christian liberation theology. Instead of judging evil deeds and condemning people for their wickedness, Kim Chi Ha justifies existence through his own power to transcend pain with love and with communal strength in resisting injustice. The poet is a passionate advocate for universal communion. *Torture Road* ends with the specter of a body in search of its imprisoned soul, and the poet's own incarceration becomes a metaphor for the whole of Korea.

Torture Road opens with an account of the poet's arrest and return to his native home. Kim Chi Ha addresses Mount Yudal and the barren yellow soil as the mother of his poem. Images of tortured ancestors are evoked and he bemoans the fact of his humiliating state of being handcuffed. The poet describes himself as "holding my grudges and crazing anger to me, the lament of my gut— . . . like a handcuffed son from the cursed land of Cholla Province and like the poet of the disdainfully treated locality. I greet you native home, to whom I have returned by the same dusty road of ten years ago. In greeting, I began to feel a smile slowly returning inside my heart."

Part II shifts abruptly (as in a movie cut) to the Korean Central Intelligence Agency (KCIA) cell. The poet links the dreadful cell to the feeling he has when waking up from a nightmare and describes the strange colored rooms as ones that "give you the illusion of some shrivelled body from remote antiquity. A body that died with an open mouth from brutal torture, hanging on the wall just as it was, decaying for several hundred years." Kim Chi Ha relates his own experience to the dead body symbolizing the history of his tragic nation. Then he describes the terrors and tortures inflicted upon himself and his friends in Section 6 at the KCIA.

The sound of footsteps,
of those hard heels, heavy on the ceiling
all night long
back and forth above me
invisible faces,
hands, and gestures

That room that shouts
and roars with laughter
that white room—
that dizziness of an abyss

Eyes widened in fright
by the agony of torn out nails
flesh ripped apart
aching and screaming to go on living
because screaming is the desire to live
the emaciated soul revives
stands along the road,
walks away

Untimely, untimely,
the friends who fell dead
into sleep covered with shame
they fell into sleep
untimely, untimely

Under whippings, kickings, sneerings
the friends who fell dead

At the end of this section, the poet calls his torment and the struggle of the Korean people for freedom the "mysterious torture road of candle light." His own confrontation with death coincides with the birth of his son, and he cries: "Oh, God, for the first time I understood your will."

In Part III of the poem, Kim Chi Ha responds to the call of life from out of the prison darkness. He speaks to another prisoner, Ha Chae Wan, and listens to his account of being tortured until his intestines ruptured. Ha Chae Wan, who had once been a tough man, speaks to the poet with phlegm-gasping breath that sounds like a ghastly echo, "like the cry of some vengeful demon." For Kim Chi Ha, the anguish of a man's suffering takes on the aspect of a supernatural wail. From a rage that makes his whole body tremble, the poet writes: "My blood calls out, refuse, refuse all lies."

Part IV of *Torture Road* begins with the proclamation of the death sentence. The poet and his friend, Kim Byong Kon, laugh when they hear these words, and Kim Byong Kon says: "This is an honor." The poet tells his friend what death means: "You are going to breathe your last breath and everything will come to an end. Flowers, wind, gentle-eyed sweethearts, the beautiful greenish smoke of supper cooking from chimneys of the foothill villages, against the full sunset. . . . All everything." The poet then asserts that they have collectively triumphed over death through the recognition of their commonly chained flesh. "It was not Kyong Sok, individually, Byong Kon, individually, or I, individually, who overcame. But all of us triumphed collectively. And triumphing, we elected the seal of eternally divine grace on our death. By accepting death, we overcame death." Kim Chi Ha recognizes that it was their common intent and mutual response to death that gave them a "collectively gained eternity."

Unlike mystics who have travelled the dark night of the soul in solitude, Kim Chi Ha's spiritual journey was made in the company of others who like himself chose truth rather than the lie that could save their life. The mystery of the spirit flashes in the poet's mind as a moment of religious, artistic, and political insight. All of the questions he has asked himself were answered in the brilliant "flame of truthful life," which burned inside the chained flesh. The spiritual ecstasy and wholeness that Kim Chi Ha experiences when overcoming death cannot be verbalized, and he states quite simply, "I began to feel as if I were in touch with the mystery of the spirit."

The last part of *Torture Road* opens with a litany that re-creates the awful monotony and rage bred by the prison:

> This waiting a long, long time, forgetting what one waits for. Just waiting, endless waiting. No other way but waiting. This waiting that drives you crazy. Waiting in hope that someone at the cost of his life, even only once . . . to smash down this waiting, vexing, blood-burning, this long, long time. Even that one small blade of grass on the prison roof does not move. That time of no wind, no sound, no color—life imprisonment.

Prison is depicted as a hell made even more terrible by the presence of an outdated Japanese cutting machine, an echo of Park Chung Hee's adoption of the refuse left by an occupying army, another metaphor for the degeneracy of the present regime. The poet mocks himself: "Welcome splendid Chi Ha, Chi Ha. Welcome to this hell. This prison is another name for your name. This hell is another name for your native earth." The prison hell of self and native land becomes a stage for shamanistic sacrifice and dismemberment. The poet offers himself: "fingernail, every strand of hair, . . . the cursed body flesh, the purged soul." In the act of offering both body and soul he becomes whole again, through a presentiment of yellow light that unites him to all people.

The poem ends with a shamanistic song.

> Dreaming,
> dreaming a bird
> become a bird and wherever
> dream madly, dream of flying.

The bird has always been a familiar of the Korean shamans, and flight is the sorcerers' traditional way of transcending themselves, as is descent, which Kim Chi Ha experienced in the prison hell. The poet chants a vision of transformation of self into all forms of being:

becomes pretty multi-colored patches
becomes a pinwheel
becomes a red tag dump glued
onto the wall of my native home
becomes the flower bier bearing the coffin
by all means, by all means
becomes a whistle wailing night train.

Kim Chi Ha brings his trance into the realm of the ordinary experience of the Korean people when he chants:

Become the singer Namchin,
become the singer Namchin
On that stage
to these crowds
I want to shout
by becoming that glittering, glittering trumpet
illuminated by stage spotlights
Hey, world!

That cry, "Hey world!" bursts the poet's throat and it is the sound of everyone who has been coerced into silence.

From this trance state, Kim Chi Ha leaves the prison gate as a bloody finger that is an empty hollow. His soul is still in the prison, and he cries out to us: "Let's go, to search for my soul. Let's go, go and open the prison gates and set my soul free. Embrace in liberation until the tears run down on my face. To unite, to be one, to be together." The poet's call is the battle cry of an agonized spirit that waits to be joined with its flesh, and the two can only unite when we struggle in common for their union. The Christ-Shaman-Poet-Healer speaks to us from his blood: "My flesh will fight until it meets with my soul. Smashed with beatings into fine, fine pieces blown away on the wind—until then, my flesh will fight."

The ancient psalmist sang: "Let truth spring from the earth" (Psalm 85:12). At no time in history has the earth been so soaked with blood, and never has the truth been so deeply buried. From the barren yellow soil of Cholla, Kim Chi Ha has reaped an awesome truth at the price of excruciating anguish and momentous sacrifice. Unless his calls are heeded by a multitude of men and women, humankind will be imprisoned in the pits we have dug for ourselves through centuries of blind faith in force. The powers that prevail have led us into atrocities and monstrous cruelty, in which people bow down before empty idols and ravage the earth with their greed. The way of Kim Chi Ha's torture road has brought forth luminous beauty and the wonder of people's power to transcend themselves through compassion and reverence for life. We have the choice of joining Kim Chi Ha in a fight to meet our souls, or succumbing to an unspeakable darkness and emptiness of heart. The poet beckons us, "Let's go, go and open the prison gates and set my soul free."

CHONG SUN KIM
SHELLY KILLEN

NOTES

1. The *Declaration of Conscience* is included in this volume.

2. The torture inflicted in 1972 on Soh Sung, charged with being a North Korean spy, involved his being hung upside down while his head and face were burned. Photographs released in Japan indicate that his face is now so scarred that it looks as if he had been burned by the heat of napalm. Soh Sung lost his ability to blink his eyes and turn his neck. A Japanese student who saw him during his trial said that Soh Sung's glasses had to be tied around his head because his ears had been burnt off. Soh Sung, a Korean born in Japan who went to Korea to study, was imprisoned for life for the "crime" of calling for unification of Korea. He was also frequently subjected to psychological torture. Kim Chi Ha was once interrogated without rest for three weeks in a room with six 500-watt electric bulbs. He later stated that this kind of torture was more unbearable than the physical ones he had undergone.

3. Wretched conditions on the Korean peninsula were partially the result of foreign invasions. *The History of Koryo* described the Mongol invasion of 1254 as follows: "This year men and women seized by the Mongol troops reached the enormous number of 206,800 and innumera-

ble people were massacred. All of the district through which the Mongol troops passed was reduced to ashes."

During the Hideyoshi invasions of the sixteenth century, more than 100,000 Japanese and Chinese troops made the peninsula their battlefield. Rice fields and towns were devastated, and hunger was so acute that the people ate the leaves from the trees. Similar stories of suffering caused by foreign powers abound in Korean history, including the Korean War, one of the most terrifying episodes that humanity has experienced. Seoul was taken and recaptured four times, as were most of the other cities on the peninsula. Vengeance was the order of the day; streets were filled with orphans and the rivers were dyed with blood.

4. Poor soil is common to the Korean land, but Cholla is an isolated agrarian center and has no cities to absorb the depressed tenant farmers. The peasantry has a long tradition of suffering exploitation at the hands of the ruling class.

5. "Kim Chi Ha's native *Cholla-Do* province has for centuries been a hotbed of revolutionary fervor. *The Yellow Dust Road* commemorates a rising of *Cholla-Do* villagers in protest against the abject circumstances of the early postwar period. *Whadang's* bamboo bushes were cut and fashioned into staves to be used against the military forces sent to quell the rebellion by the Syngman Rhee government. The fires ignited on *Opo* Hill signalled the start of the uprising, in which one-third of the village's six hundred farmers were massacred alongside *Pujuu* Brook" (Kim Chi Ha, *Cry of the People and Other Poems* [Kanagawa-Ken, Japan: Autumn Press, 1974], p. 25).

6. In 1945, Korea was liberated from the Japanese colonial rule. Since the liberation was not the result of Korean efforts, it had ominous consequences. Korea became a victim of the cold war and was divided into two parts. Despite certain differences in detail, the United States assumed Japan's imperial role in Asia after the latter's defeat in the Pacific War. As a part of an imperial maneuver, the United States brought Syngman Rhee back to Korea from his exile as the U.S.-approved leader of South Korea. *The New York Times*, June 27, 1950, said that the perpetuation of Rhee's rule was "based on total dependence on the U.S., that is to say, on the U.S.A.'s economic, political and military support." Rhee's regime was marked by anticommunist frenzy, police brutality, electoral fraud, bribery, and other vices. His many years of repressive rule survived because of U.S. support; it was Rhee who appealed for U.S. military intervention when the Korean War erupted on June 25, 1950.

Rhee's continual repression and the economic miseries of the period reached such proportions that in 1960 there were mass student demonstrations. The U.S. government subsequently decided to depose Rhee because his stubborn, anti-Japanese stance had become an obstacle to the development of U.S. foreign policy in Asia.

7. Korea was surrounded by powerful neighbors and placed in the position of a pawn in the chess games of China, Japan, northern nomads,

and later the United States. Since antiquity, the Korean people have been victims of colonial rule and of unwanted foreign warfare on Korean soil. The earliest colonial rule goes back as far as the second century B.C., when a four-hundred year subjugation by China began. In the sixth century A.D., China tried to colonize Korea again and repeatedly attacked Koguryo, one of the Korean kingdoms at that time. Both the Sui and the T'ang empires' campaigns against Koguryo continued for more than a half century, and on one occasion China dispatched one million soldiers to the peninsula. Although the country was finally unified in the seventh century, northern nomadic invasions and Japanese attacks continued to devastate the land and bring hardship to the people. Korea often received Chinese military aid to repel these attacks. This assistance served to bring more wars to the peninsula.

Ironically, the Silla Kingdom, which first unified the peninsula, relied upon Chinese aid for this achievement. Korea assumed the weak role of dependency in the unification process. Korean history reveals that reliance upon foreign powers for solutions to internal problems invited one tragedy after another. Reliance on China (and later the United States), known as the *sadae* (serve the larger), contributed to the loss of national identity, through the upper class aping of the Chinese (later the Americans) and the accruing of debts to China. Although Korea maintained some measures of independence through appeasement, Korea as a tributary state of China became the latter's semi-colony.

The foreign domination culminated in the Japanese occupation of the peninsula between 1910 and 1945. During the Japanese colonial rule, Korea was administered by the Japanese secret police and the military sword. The Koreans were unable to publish newspapers in their own language or teach Korean culture and history. They were coerced into worshipping the Japanese emperor and forced to change their names to the Japanese style. They were also prohibited from speaking Korean in the schools and public places. The Japanese military government seized vast amounts of land from the Korean peasants through fraudulent land investigation. They also took over fishery rights, timber and mining rights, and communications and forests.

Standing at the crossroads of the powers, the Koreans were bred on *sadae*—the colonial mentality of flattering the strong and bullying the weak—which became fatal to Korea's autonomous growth and inner development. Long years of colonial rule divided them and taught them to hate themselves. They also nurtured bitterness, insecurity, and helplessness. Fear and mistrust led to a defensive posture, which bred more feuds and the elimination of opposition by brute force. No individual was able to counter this self-defeating system with a program for reform that could forge a pluralistic society.

Korea managed to survive as a political entity, but remained a society haunted by fanaticism. The country was continually polarized into an oppressed peasant populace and an extremely selfish governing elite. The parasitical and corrosive character of the ruling class was such that the Korean peasants in the Yi Dynasty gave up the development of their own resources. Chong Yangyong (1762–1836), the great scholar of the period, tells how distortion and abuse by officials ruthlessly shattered any "constructive" productive relationship in Korea. His story tells us about the general temper of traditional Korean society: "Some sixty-seven districts of the southern seacoast were known for their abundant tangerine production, but the trees were gradually destroyed during a period of ten to twenty years, due to the severe appropriation by officials. Early every autumn, provincial officials came to the orchards with records to count the precise number of green tangerines on each tree. When the tangerines were ripe, officials came to recount them, and forced the owners to pay for any tangerines which had either been lost or blown off by the wind. In such cases the owners were forced to supplement the shortage of tangerines with money or produce, or even to provide expensive cooking chickens and pigs. Therefore, the owners of the trees were unable to bear the legal abuse of these political parasites, and finally made holes in the roots of the tangerine trees and put the powder of peppers in them to cause them to wither away" (*Mongmin Simso,* trans. Won Ch'ang-gyu [Seoul, 1956], pp. 213–14).

8. In the ninth century a Korean king issued a decree to regulate and control, in accordance with class distinction, the quality and type of turbans, trousers, boots, socks, blankets, belts, hats, and vests. The state could decide which social stratum should use which type of cow bits, muzzles, stirrups, saddle-cushions, and cart seats. The length and width of individual houses, the quality and grade of ells, ceilings, eaves, walls, fences, flagstones, platforms, and gates were also subject to governmental control. The character of this social control can be seen from an edict in which the state had the right to regulate the kind of underwear that was worn. The eighth-century Village Register of the Silla period further indicates the extreme poverty and marked severity of social control. The census had detailed accounts of land distribution, rank of household, and rank of labor force for military, state treasury, and public works. It also included detailed lists of animals and nut-bearing trees raised or planted by individuals. The tightness of the Korean bureaucracy has been a source of extreme frustration that produced an aggression that turned back on itself.

9. According to the *Samguk Yusa* (one of the Korean ancient chronicles), a man named Hyangduk lived in Ungch'onju on a little farm. In the eighth century, a famine struck the land so badly that the soil could yield no crop. Hyangduk's father nearly starved to death. Hyangduk cut some flesh from his thigh and fed the old man.

10. In spite of foreign invasions and acute oppression, the Korean people have sustained their struggle for freedom and independence and tried to maintain their integrity and identity. There are numerous examples of protest and resistance movements in the past. The current spirit of

liberation theology is embodied in the character of Kim Chi Ha and the many other men and women who have been imprisoned for bearing witness to the truth.

11. For example, the *Samguk Sagi* (ancient Korean chronicle) says that King Chich'ollo had a phallus measuring over one foot five inches. His noblemen found him a bird seven feet five inches tall, in order that his exceptional anatomy might have a female counterpart.

12. Kim Chi Ha said in his *Declaration of Conscience:* "I regard myself as a free thinker not bound by any ideological system. I hope my ideas are neither shaped by personal ambition nor yield to intimidation and that they are also unfettered by any dogma or creed. Thus I have never defined myself as an adherent of any 'ism.' I belong in the creative tension formed by the chaos of freedom. . . . So far I have never found one system of thought that was logically convincing. I am still searching. In a sense, this is a shameful admission, but there are extenuating circumstances, I think."

13. Park was an officer in the Japanese army during the Pacific War and was elevated to the rank of company commander because of his exceptional devotion and dedication to the Japanese Emperor against his own people. Once he had secured Washington's sanction as a reliable anti-communist leader, he kept a tight grip on the populace and set up a state even more repressive than Syngman Rhee's. The Korean Central Intelligence Agency became the eyes and ears of his dictatorship, and the country was organized into a vast network of spies, informers, and terrorists.

To justify his attacks upon all who criticized his regime, Park created the anti-communist laws and many other emergency measures in the guise of protecting the country from communism. During Syngman Rhee's time and the Korean War, most Communists in the south were virtually eradicated. In actuality, there were no Communists left to whom the law could apply. The anti-communist laws have been used against students, liberal intellectuals, and Christians who verbalized dissent.

Park supports a regime that is as monstrous and repressive as Joseph Stalin's at its pitch point of paranoia. Just as Hitler built concentration camps and supported murder in the name of national crisis, Park masks his frenzied drive for absolute power and his complicity with U.S. and Japanese business investors with the cover-up of protecting the country from "subversives." The foreign companies that took advantage of South Korea's anti-union and anti-strike laws set up assembly factories in the country; workers living on starvation wages turn out finished products to be sold in Asia and the United States at low prices. Although some degree of economic progress has been made in cities, Korean peasants, who comprise one-half of the population, remain impoverished.

In a certain respect, Korea has remained a colonial nation, manipulated by imperial powers for the exploitation of cheap labor. In the nineteenth century, the imperialists physically occupied territories and extracted raw materials from them; modern world powers use corporate agreement in the form of monetary loans to bind the people. The military and police have been consistently used as a shield to protect foreign investments in Korea, as they have been in other Third World countries.

The maintenance of 40,000 U.S. troops in Korea costs the American people $700 million annually. Their presence on the militarily tense Korean peninsula constitutes a "tripwire" that could propel the United States into automatic combat should a new war break out in Korea—leaving few, if any, options for U.S. policymakers. Even more alarming is the fact that these troops operate under a nuclear shield that may consist of as many as 686 nuclear weapons, according to recent estimates from the Center for Defense Information, including artillery shells, missile warheads, bombs, and landmines. Over the past year, the Pentagon has threatened the possible "first use" of nuclear weapons in the event of a new war in Korea, further intensifying the already supercharged tension on the peninsula.

Biography of Kim Chi Ha

1941: Born on *February 4* at Mokp'o, South Cholla Province. Kim Chi Ha was the only male child. His given name was Kim Yongil.

1953: Graduated from Sanjong Grammar School in Mokp'o. Entered Mokp'o Middle School.

1954: The family moved to Wonju, Kangwon Province, when Kim Chi Ha's father was offered work as a film technician. Kim Chi Ha transferred to the Wonju Middle School.

1956: Graduated from Wonju Middle School.

1959: Graduated from Seoul Chungdong High School. Entered the Department of Aesthetics of Liberal Arts College, Seoul National University.

1960: Participated in the April 19th Student Revolution, which toppled the Syngman Rhee regime. *November:* participated in the conference for the initiation of National Unification League of Seoul National University.

1961: *May 4:* National Unification League of Seoul National University proposed South and North Student Conference for the Unification of Korea. *May 5:* Kim Chi Ha organized the Preparatory Committee Conference of All Nations Student League for National Unification. The promotion for national unification was centered around Seoul National University, and Kim Chi Ha was a prime figure in the movement. *May 13:* About five thousand students and Seoulites opened a conference for "Determination to Promote National Unification and the Welcoming of South and North Student Conference." There was a march through the city under the slogans: "Let's go to the North," "Come to the South," "Let's meet at Panmunjom." *May 16:* General Park Chung Hee initiated a military coup and arrested leaders of the student movement. Kim Chi Ha ended his studies and went underground. The poet also contracted tuberculosis while working on the docks and in the coal mines.

1963: *March:* Kim Chi Ha returned to the university.

1964: Joined the movement in opposition to the Korea-Japan Conference, which would have fostered Korean economic dependence upon Japan. Drafted many proclamations against the Korea-Japan treaty at Seoul National University.

1965: In *June* the Japanese-South Korean Normalization Treaty was ratified and Park proclaimed martial law. He mobilized six divisions to oppress the opposition. Kim Chi Ha again went underground.

1966: Graduated from the Department of Aesthetics at Seoul National University. Hospitalized for a year in Seoul West Gate Hospital because of deteriorating condition of TB.

1969: Published the following poems: *Yellow Dust Road*, *Rain*, *Light Load*, *Green Bean Flower*, *The Plain*. All of the poems appeared in the magazine *The Poet*.

1970: Published *Five Bandits* in the monthly magazine *The World of Ideas* (May issue). It is satirical poetry about the injustice and corruption of the privileged classes in South Korea. The poem also appeared in the New People's Party magazine, *Democratic Front*. Park arrested Kim Chi Ha and the editors of *The World of Ideas* and *Democratic Front* on the grounds that they had violated the Anti-Communist Law and had helped propaganda activities in North Korea. Both publications were banned. Due to the deteriorating condition of his tuberculosis, Kim Chi Ha was bailed out of prison. In *May*, the play *Napoleon Cognac* was performed at Ewha Women's University. Kim Chi Ha was director of his own play, but before the curtain went up he was imprisoned because of the publication of *Five Bandits*. The play was acted without the director. *December:* Kim Chi Ha published his first collection of poems, *Yellow Land*, a work that embodied the essence of his feelings toward Korea.

1971: *March:* The poem *Divine Wind of Castor Bean*, which was critical of the Japanese writer Mishima Yukio, appeared in the monthly magazine *Bridge*. *April:* Kim Chi Ha became active in the Farmers' Cooperative Movement in his native province. The movement was led by the Catholic church. His plays *Napoleon Cognac* and *Copper Yi Sunsin* were to be presented in Sogang University, but due to government interference they were cancelled. The poem *Song of the Cherry Bandit* was published in the July issue of *Bridge*. *October:* Organized six hundred Catholics in his native province for a demonstration for the Realization of Social Justice. This advanced the activities of the student movement and he again went underground, as many students were arrested.

1972: Kim Chi Ha's long poem *Groundless Rumors* was published in the Catholic monthly *Creation* in the April issue. The Park government banned the magazine and both the editor and publisher were arrested. *April 12:* Kim Chi Ha went into hiding and then was arrested by the KCIA. During this time the KCIA arrested 170 writers, professors, and students, who were interrogated and tortured to determine the whereabouts of Kim Chi Ha. *April 27:* The government placed Kim Chi Ha in the National Masan Sanatorium. This was actually a form of imprisonment, since he was under constant surveillance. *July 15:* Kim Chi Ha left the sanatorium.

1973: *May:* Kim Chi Ha married the daughter of writer Pak Kyungri.

1974: Went underground again after Park Chung Hee proclaimed Emergency Measures Numbers One And Two. *April 3:* Kim Chi Ha's *Cry of the People* spread through Korea in the form of anonymous leaflets. They were confiscated with the proclamation of Emergency Measure Number Four. The English daily newspaper *The Guardian*, *Time* magazine, and Japan's *Yomiuri* newspaper pointed out that *Cry of the People* had been written by Kim Chi Ha. Autumn Press in Japan printed an English edition of Kim Chi Ha's *Cry of the People and Other Poems. April 19:* Kim Chi Ha's son was born. *April 25:* Arrested on Hoksan Island while working as an assistant director of the film *Blue Girl. June 27:* He was subjected to a military court martial and stated that the sooner the government power retreated, the better it would be for the restoration of human dignity. *July 13:* Accused of violation of Emergency Measure Number Four, violation of the National Security Law, and instigating revolt. He was sentenced to death. *July 20:* The death sentence was commuted to life imprisonment. An International Committee to Save Kim Chi Ha was formed, including such well known figures as Jean Paul Sartre, Howard Zinn, and Noam Chomsky.

1975: *February 15:* Released from Yongdongp'o Prison. He said "time and tide flow like the water, and either time and the tide are crazy or I am." Kim Chi Ha's release was totally unexpected. On *February 24* he stated in the newspaper, "I am not yet released." *February 25–27:* His prison diary, *Torture Road . . . 1974*, was published in the Tong-A Ilbo newspaper. *March 13:* Arrested by the Seoul police shortly after a visit with his mother-in-law. *March 14:* Jailed by the KCIA on the grounds that he had violated Article Four of the Anti-Communist Law. *March 20:* Tortured into admitting that he was a Communist. The government printed ninety thousand copies of this statement and sent it throughout Korea, Japan, and the United States. *June 29:* Received Lotus award from the Third World Writers Conference. The members of the conference sent a letter to Park Chung Hee calling for release of Kim Chi Ha; they stated that he was one of the outstanding poets in the world, a symbol for democracy and freedom.

Recommended for the Nobel Literature and Peace Prizes. On *August 4* his *Declaration of Conscience* was smuggled out of prison. Theologians throughout the world signed a letter to Park asking for his release and stating how deeply moved they were by Kim Chi Ha's integrity and Christian conscience. *December 25:* The entire works of Kim Chi Ha were published by the Korean publishing company Hanyangsa in Japan.

1976: Kim Chi Ha tried in the Seoul District Court on *December 23.* The poet spoke without notes from 6:45 to 9:50 P.M. and began his testimony by thanking the prosecutor for requesting a ten-year sentence in addition to the life sentence he was given in an earlier trial. Seven years were added on to Kim Chi Ha's life sentence.

1977: *November:* Amnesty International reports that Kim Chi Ha is still being held in solitary confinement in Seoul's West Gate Prison.

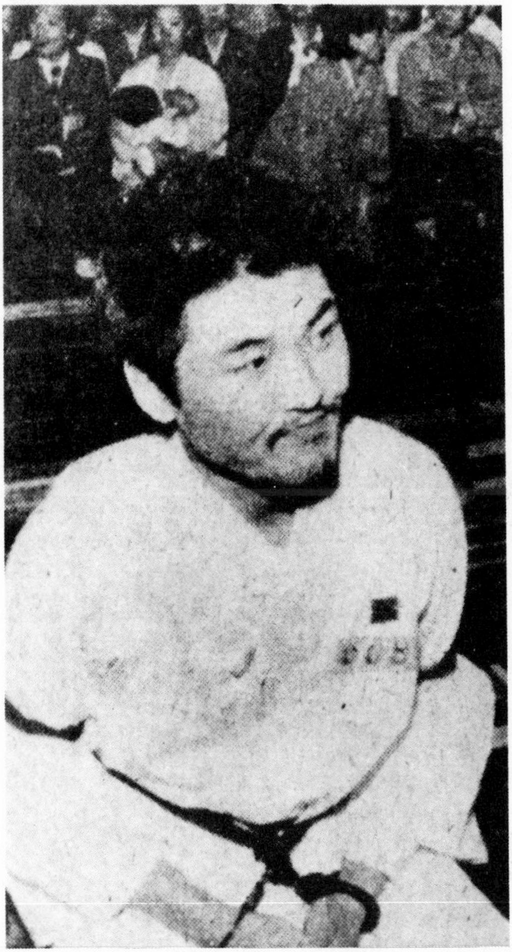

Kim Chi Ha at his trial, May 19, 1975

Prayer

Midnight, December 25, 1974

Prayer! Prayer! Prayer!
May heaven accept this prayer of mine
repeated over and over again for many months.
May the edge of my soul become sharper.
Even if my breast explodes in agonized wailing,
let me set out for the distant battlefield.
Let me set out on this journey.
Let me go out into the wilderness,
into the land that nearly drives me mad
with its awakening bitterness,
the land over which stars sparkle
in the frozen winter dawn.
Let me pray alone,
let me decide alone:
to be with the masses, at the bottom,
to be beaten with them,
to decay with them,
and finally to rise up gallantly from the earth with them
in the bright morning sunshine,
with our heads held high.

. . . into the wilderness

Mount Chiri

When I see that snow-capped mountain
My blood begins to boil
When I see the groves of green bamboo
Anger stokes the coals of inner pain
For even now
Beneath the bamboo tree
Beneath the mountain
My kinsman's blood is running down

Oh, that field
That curve of mountain range
Overflowing with blood
And so it weeps

The banner
The blazing eyes
The glare of white clothes*
Worn on departure to war

Moaning, moaning
They cry as they embrace
Their ancient, endless poverty
With single-handled rusty scythe

Behind them they have left
Their unkept promises of return
But somehow they shall come home

*White clothes here represent Korean peasants.

Oh, you who have departed
And you whose silent tears
Are deep within my heart

Beneath the frozen sky of winter
Men have left from here
Just as the water of the river flows
To here they will return as spirits
Just as the water of the river flows

The sound of their cries
Wounds me so sharply
Oh, those ancient songs

When I see that snow-capped mountain
My blood begins to boil
When I see the groves of green bamboo
Anger stokes the coals of inner pain

Oh, the rage that will not die
Rage that pounds against me like the waves

Oh, Mount Chiri
Oh, Mount Chiri

—Translated by Chong Sun Kim and Shelly Killen

Seoul

Where the sword stands high
Where heavy fog blankets its hilt
Where one can never see the blood
That seeped throughout the night

Where the sword stands high
And gleams deep blue
Against the daylight

Where all your grappling
Will never give you a hold
Where your foot will never
Go down safely on the earth
And you will never know
Where you are
How to go
How to leave
You will never leave
No hands shall unearth
You from this grave

Oh, this marsh
This cursed land
Where the swords stand
Like a forest
Against the sky

I pray that I may overcome you
I pray that I may overcome you

Oh, Seoul

We sacrifice all
All of our souls
Beneath your sword

I offer you my empty body
I offer you my flesh
All
Burned away in withered rebellions
With no wind to stir them

All that is left
Is to fall
One last chance
To fall

On that sword
On that sword
Like a red, red flower

Dying
To overcome you
By any means

Dying
With my blood
To forever rust
Your sword

—Translated by Chong Sun Kim and Shelly Killen

The Road

So hard to walk
This wretched road
Yet it's here where
You must walk

I want to delay it
Yet there is no way
To allay the awful journey

Unfulfilled yearnings
Melancholic songs
All that remains
Unsaid, unfinished

But . . .

This is the road
We must walk on
And our thoughts
Must go onward

Tears are coming down
Tears are coming down

You must live on here
You must forget here
You with your two eyes
Cannot see at all
I with my mouth
Cannot speak at all

But . . .

This is the road
We must walk on
And our thoughts
Must go onward

—Translated by Chong Sun Kim and Shelly Killen

"Go ahead and make them laugh
Because we are two-bit circus men"

Rope Walker

I'm on the rope
On the tightrope
I have walked
For thirty years
If I survive this
I will walk again
If I'm reborn I will
Walk in eternity

Sharper than a blade
Deeper than sleep
The pain of empty space
The pain of walking alone

Hey, Drummer
T'odorak t'ak t'ak
Go ahead and make them laugh
Because we are two-bit circus men

From your father
And your grandfather
From Hwagae to eternity
From Namch'ang* to the corner
Of some dim back alley
Until the very last act of
Dying and vomiting blood

*Both Hwagae and Namch'ang are place names.

We are two-bit circus men
And you know
Dying is really wonderful
Because it only happens once

Walk, walk that tightrope
Walk right, walk left
Walk sky, walk earth
They are all our hells
And we must walk on them

There is no other way
Damn it
There is no other way
So walk the rope

You have bet your life
On your feet
In just this space
It was decided at birth

Look drummer
Chonggi, chonggi, chongchuk'kung
May there be many spectators
For we are two-bit circus men
And the ones who watch us had
Better be cold-blooded types

And even if we die
Are torn to pieces
Vomit our blood
We shall make them laugh
Because you know
Dying is really wonderful
Since it only happens once.

—Translated by Chong Sun Kim and Shelly Killen

A Declaration of Conscience

(Kim Chi Ha wrote this manuscript while in Seoul's West Gate prison, from the beginning to the middle of May 1975. He entrusted it to a prisoner who was about to be released, and at the beginning of June it was given to Father Hyon Jung Youn, a Catholic priest. Father Youn gave it to a visiting foreign priest at the beginning of July. This priest sent it to Father James Sinnott, M.M., in the United States.)

To all who love justice and truth.

The Park regime is tying me up in a conspiratorial net of incredible lies. They say I am a Communist who infiltrated the Catholic church and pretended to be an advocate of democracy and human rights. I have been arrested and imprisoned on these charges.

The regime will soon begin a courtroom charade to "legally" brand me forever as a "treacherous Marxist-Leninist agent." I will be forced into the ranks of that legion of government-designated "Communists."

I am not the only target of this conspiracy. It is directed at the whole movement to restore democracy and at the Christian churches which have been fighting for social justice. The government is particularly determined to label as pro-Communist the National Priests Association for the Realization of Justice, the National Council for the Restoration of Democracy, and all youth and student movements. This scheme is the forerunner of a broad crackdown on dissent.

The government has been making these vile charges against me for more than a decade; they are nothing new. I should prefer not to waste words with a personal defense here. The Korean Central Intelligence Agency (KCIA) agents say, "If you have a statement to make about these charges, do it in court." For once I agreed with them. I intended to do just that: to try to bring out some of the truth about this travesty of justice during the trial by challenging the prosecutor.

However, the current political situation compels me to speak out now. It is not just my convictions and my credibility that are endangered. The net has been thrown widely to encompass all democratic forces, my church, and the student movement. I have an obligation to history and to my people to state my beliefs and the facts about my arrest as I know them.

AM I A COMMUNIST?

I have never in the past thought of myself as a Communist, and I still do not. I am not a Communist. The KCIA charges against me are patently absurd. My lawyer has told me they have taken the "confession" I was forced to write and have made it public to prove that I am a Communist. The "confession" in the pamphlet is called Statement No. 2, but actually it was the third one. The KCIA discarded the second statement but still numbered the third version as No. 2. These details aside, it is true that the document was written by my hand, but not by my mind and soul. It was not a voluntary statement.

I was a powerless individual in an underground interrogation room of the KCIA's Fifth Bureau. They were the almighty agency of state terror, beyond any law or decency. How much truth do you think there is in those sheets of paper called my "confession"? From the time of my arrest I was pressured to say that I was a "Communist who had infiltrated the Catholic church." The government had decided to destroy me politically and religiously. They were going to crush me until I was flattened out like a piece of dried cuttlefish. I resisted my interrogators and refused to "confess." The grilling continued for five or six days, I think. Finally, they wore me down. I had not been in good health before my arrest; I had fainted several times due to lack of sleep, poor food, and extreme exhaustion. The constant questioning left me even more exhausted and delirious. For a number of nights, I was kept awake all night long. I knew the Park regime would use any means necessary to convict me as a Communist. It did no good to keep telling the interrogators that I was innocent. They had strict orders from higher-ups to "get Kim Chi Ha" regardless of the facts. The KCIA agents were cogs in the machine; they could not refuse that order. They hammered away at me day and night. Without sleep and in ill health, I could not continue this nerve-wracking war of attrition and I violated my conscience.

Finally, on the sixth day, I wrote out a statement which they dictated. I scribbled it down like graffiti on a toilet wall and threw it at them. That is how my "confession" was written.

As one might expect, the statement is filled with lies and inconsistencies. It has all the stock phrases so dear to the KCIA hacks: "I became a Communist out of a sense of inferiority and frustration due to poverty and illness."[1] This is the vilest part of the document. They used the same phrasing over and over again when I was indicted in 1970 for writing *Five Bandits*, for *Groundless Rumors* in 1972, and in the National Federation of Youth and Students incident in 1974. There is a materialistic determinism in the phraseology, as if all the poor and afflicted are "potential carriers of the disease of communism." Would any self-respecting person write such craven drivel of his own free will?

According to the "confession," all my activities, including writing *Five Bandits* and *Groundless Rumors*, were due to my communist ideas. I wonder if foreign readers of these poems were deceived by my communist propaganda? There must be many red faces among those foreign literary critics who praised my work and did not even realize that it was "communist propaganda." If *Five Bandits* is communist literature, why have the charges against me been pending for more than four years? And why was I not even indicted for *Groundless Rumors?*

The "confession" says that I am a Communist *and* a Catholic. That is a contradiction much like being a "democratic fascist." Every schoolchild knows that Marx regarded religion, especially Christianity, as the "opium of the people." The "confession" is filled with such nonsense.

I understand that the KCIA pamphlet cites a few books I had in my possession as "proof" that I am a Communist. They are so stupid! Their petty, frightened police-state minds! No matter how severely intellectual freedom is restricted in South Korea, does reading a few Marxist classics make a person a Communist? The most avid readers of leftist books are the censors who check every piece of literature that comes into this country. If they can read those materials, why is it a crime for me? I have read hundreds of books; the government seized fewer than ten. Every one of those without exception is regarded as a classic in other countries and scholars are required to read them.

The KCIA reproduces some of the notes I jotted down in prison from April 1974 until February 1975. Again, those memorandums and notes are supposed to be "proof" that I am a Communist. Those notes contain all kinds of thoughts and emotions. Ideas that flitted into my mind like birds flitting past my cell window. There are ruminations on this or that, outlines of projects that I hope to write about in the future. Bits and pieces, unconnected fragments. They do not show that I am a man ideologically committed to communism. If the government will make public *all* my notes, the charges against me will fall of their own weight. Anyone who examines the materials will see my values: my hatred of oppression and exploitation, my groping in the political wilderness for a way out of these inequities, how I have driven myself in the quest for answers! This search has nothing to do with communism.

How should I define my ideological position? Before I attempt that, two points require clarification.

First, I regard myself as a free thinker not bound by any ideological system. I hope my ideas are neither shaped by personal ambition nor yield to intimidation and that they are also unfettered by any dogma or creed. Thus I have never defined myself as an adherent of any "ism." I belong in the creative tension formed by the chaos of freedom. A natural pool swirls with cross currents of ideas, values, systems, and experiences. By diving into that pool again and again I hope to come up with a few grains of truth. I stand beside that pool poised for the next dive.

Secondly, I am ideologically unfinished. That's a crude way of saying that I have never accepted one ideology as my operative value system. So far I have never found one system of thought that was logically convincing. I am still searching. In a sense, this is a shameful admission, but there are extenuating circumstances, I think. An individual's beliefs and conscience must be free, and the process that shapes them must also be open, competitive, and eclectic. People have a natural right to find their own values. Even the Yushin Constitution, promulgated by Park Chung Hee in December 1972, guarantees this right to South Korean society. Nevertheless, intellectual life and value formulation are totally controlled in our country. A single ideology with its priorities, preferences, taboos, and sanctions is dominant.

Consider the spiritual ethos of South Korea. The flow of information is controlled. One can only read a limited number of authorized books. Anti-intellectualism and pervasive secrecy are the rule. I have tried, often with doubts and remorse, to find the truth in this darkness. I am not the only one. Every South Korean who has sought to understand what is going on in this country and in the world has trod the same uncertain, dangerous path. My ideological education is incomplete.

Under these conditions surely there is virtually no possibility of "spontaneous communism" sprouting here. Our conditioned reflex to "Communists" was to imagine red-faced devils with horns growing out of their heads and long claws dripping with blood. Every South Korean below the age of thirty has been educated and indoctrinated this way. Furthermore, we have never been taught anything about communism except emotional diatribes against it. Even if a few curious people secretly read some leftist books, how could they turn into full-fledged Communists with a firm grasp of dialectics, party history, and doctrine? No "spontaneous Communist" could emerge from the younger generation. That includes me. Far from being a committed Communist, as the KCIA charges, I have no reliable information about the nature of communism or what life is like in a communist country. The charge that I am a Communist is utterly groundless.

DEMOCRACY, REVOLUTION, VIOLENCE

I want to identify with the oppressed, the exploited, the troubled, and the despised. I want my love to be dedicated, passionate, and manifested in practical ways. This is the totality of my self-imposed task for humanity, the alpha and the omega of my intellectual search. I hope that my odyssey will be understood as a love for humankind.

My desire to love all people as my brothers and sisters makes me hate the oppression and exploitation that dehumanizes life. Those who exploit others dehumanize themselves. Thus I fight against oppression and exploitation; the struggle is my existence.

I became a Catholic because Catholicism conveys a universal message. Not only the spiritual and material burdens could be lifted from people but also oppression itself could be ended by the salvation of *both* the oppressor and the oppressed. Catholicism is capable of assimilating and synthesizing these contradictory and conflicting ideologies, theories, and value standards into a universal truth.

My beliefs spring from a confident love for the common people. I have opposed the Park regime and ridiculed the "Five Bandits" because they are the criminal gangsters looting this country. I have grown up as one of the oppressed masses. That perspective enabled me to see that a pernicious, elitist bias permeates our society. The oppressors say the masses are base, ugly, morally depraved, innately lazy, untrustworthy, ignorant, and a spiritless inferior race. But the common people I have known are not like that. They are honest and industrious. They may look stupid to a Seoul bureaucrat, but they are endowed with a rich, native intelligence. Although they seem listless, they possess enormous inner strength and determination. They may be rough and not very sophisticated, but they have genuine affection for their friends and neighbors. The common people I knew are proud, full of an unassuming vitality.

I have total confidence in the people. Given the opportunity, they will find correct solutions to their problems. And their time is coming. The people cannot be denied their rights and justice much longer. My confidence in the people has led me to trust their ability to determine their own fate.

Those who fear the people, who find the masses despicable, are not democrats. When the going gets rough, they will stand at the side of tyranny.

What is democracy? It is an ideology opposed to silence, a system that respects a free logos and freedom of speech. It encourages the cacophony of dissent. A political system where everything is not revealed to the public is not a democracy. I believe that the truth, only the truth, will liberate people. A public consciousness dulled by soporific incantations and smothered in darkness can only be liberated by the truth. Only when the people struggle out of the darkness, driven along by the very chaos of their opposition to tyranny, will they reach the sun-drenched fields. Then they can head toward Canaan, the land of justice and freedom promised by the Creator. This is my dream, my faith.

I cannot describe this Promised Land in detail. No one person can do that. I think it will be created by the collective effort of all the people. My task is to fight on until the people hold in their own hands the power to shape their destiny. I want a victory for real democracy, complete freedom of speech. Nothing more, nothing less. In this sense, I am a radical democrat and libertarian. I am also a Catholic, one of the oppressed citizens of the Republic of Korea, and a young man who loathes privilege, corruption, and dictatorial power. This defines my political beliefs. I have nothing more to add.

Democracy does not require a "benevolent ruler who loves the people." A ruler who fears the people's wrath and weapons is preferable. Democracy entails an uncompromising rejection of oppression. There is no democracy as long as the people cannot depose an undesirable ruler. Thus, democracy does not deny the people the right of revolution; on the contrary, that fundamental right is the last guarantee of popular sovereignty. This self-evident truth must never be forgotten.

The right of revolution, the constant and eternal possibility of overthrowing illegitimate authority, is the ultimate sanction against misrule that enables the people to defend themselves from oppression and exploitation. Tyrants, of course, make revolution illegal; even discussion of it is banned as subversive. Thus they can continue their political and economic dominations. But that is why I must support resistance and revolution.

I feel enormous pride in our Korean traditions. The people have often protested against injustice and misgovernment. Unfortunately, the rulers, irredeemably callous and arrogant, often crushed the protests with force. Under these circumstances have the people any choice but revolution?

Catholic political thought since Thomas Aquinas has explicitly recognized the people's right and duty, based on natural law, to overthrow a tyrant who threatens their existence and common good. Resistance abruptly changes the course of human affairs. The people themselves recover their humanity. The masses undergo a sudden and profound awakening; history makes up for lost time by encouraging the people to miraculous feats.

Sooner or later resistance and revolution lead to the phenomenon of violence. When the violence of authority sustains oppression, the people's will is crushed, their best leaders are killed, and the rest are cowed into submission. The "silence of law and order" settles grimly across the land. Then an antithetical situation exists where violence must shatter this macabre order. To a degree, I approve of this kind of violence. I must approve of it. I reject the violence of oppression and accept the violence of resistance. I reject dehumanizing violence and accept the violence that restores human dignity. It could justly be called a "violence of love."

Jesus used his whip on the merchants defiling the temple. That was the "violence of love." It was force suffused with love. Jesus wanted the afflicted *and* their oppressive rulers to be reborn again as true children of God.

Violence and destructiveness obviously bring suffering and hardship. But we must sometimes cause and endure suffering. Never is this more true than when the people are dozing in silent submission, when they cannot be awakened from their torpor. To preach "nonviolence" at such a time leaves them defenseless before their enemies. When the people must be awakened and sent resolutely off to battle, violence is unavoidable. Gandhi and Frantz Fanon agonized over this dilemma. Father Camilo Torres took a rifle and joined the people. He died with them, the weapon never fired. The fallen priest with his rifle epitomized godliness. I do not know if his beliefs and methods were correct or not, but the purity of his love always moves me to tears. He staggered along his road to Golgotha with uncertain tread. He was prepared to commit a sin out of a love for others. He was not afraid to burn in the depths of eternal hell.

True nonviolence requires total noncompliance and noncooperation. It concedes nothing to the oppressors. The superficial kind of nonviolence, which makes limited gestures of opposition, is just another form of craven cooperation with the oppressors. Cowardly nonviolence is morally equivalent to cruel violence because with both the people get crushed. On the other hand, the "violence of love" is essentially the same as a "courageous nonviolence" in that it arms the people against their foes. I approve of the "violence of love" but I am also a proponent of true nonviolence.

The revolution I support will be a synthesis of true nonviolence and an agonized violence of love. (I am now working on a long ballad, *Chang Il Tam*, set against this background.)

To reach that golden mean—a nonviolence that does not drift to cowardly compromise and a violence that does not break the bonds of love and lapse into carnage—humankind must undergo an unceasing spiritual revival and the masses must experience a universal self-awakening.

While I grant that the violence of Blanquism* can light the psychological fuse to revolution, I do not anticipate or sup-

*The revolutionary doctrine that a socialist state can be established only by an immediate seizure of power by the workers themselves.

port a "lucky revolution" achieved by a small number of armed groups committing terrorist acts of violence. That is why I have eschewed the formation of or membership in secret organizations and have participated in activities consistent with the democratic process: writing and petitions, rallies, and prayer meetings.

My vision of a revolution is the creation of a unified Korea based on freedom, democracy, self-reliance, and peace. More fundamentally, however, it must enable the Korean people to decide their own fate. I can confidently support such a revolution.

That revolution will not follow foreign models or patterns, but flow from our unique revolutionary tradition. The Tong Hak rebellion,[2] the March First Independence Movement, and the 1960 April Student Revolution foreshadow the next revolution.

THE DREAM OF A REVOLUTIONARY RELIGION: THE WORLD OF "CHANG IL TAM"

The more I search for answers, the more contradictory ideas I find and the more confused I am. J. B. Metz confessed to the same experience. Yet the antagonistic diversity of these systems of thought makes me strive even more for faith in the one unique, absolute being. I believe such faith is attainable.

Must revolution reject religion and religion be the foe of revolution? I think the answer is No. Perhaps by this reply alone I could not be a Marxist-Leninist. But the Marxist dictum that religion is the opiate of the masses is only a partial truth applicable to one aspect of religion.

When a people has been brutally misruled and exploited for a long time, they lose their passion for justice and their affection for other people. Committed only to self-survival, they lapse into an individualistic materialism. Their near-crazed resentment and rage at social and economic conditions, diverted into frustration and self-hatred, is repeatedly dissipated in fragmented, anomic actions. Our prisons are full of lower-class criminals, thrown there by a ruling elite that spits on the poor and flourishes on social injustice. The prisoners' roster of crimes is diverse: armed robbery, theft, murder, desertion from military service, kidnapping, etc. Yet their wretched tragedy has a common origin in frustration and isolation.

The chief priests and Pharisees defuse the people's bitter resentment and moral indignation with sentimental charity. The people are emasculated by mercy. The god of philanthropy serves the oppressor by turning people into a mob of beggars. That is why I cannot admire Albert Schweitzer.

In similar situations of bondage and deprivation, prophetic religions of love arise in the wilderness and shake the emotions of the oppressed and mistreated people. The slumbering masses awaken like a thunderclap; their human and divine qualities suddenly shine forth. This is the mystery of resurrection—this is revolution. That resurrection fashions people in God's image, opens their eyes to their own dignity and turns their frustration and self-hatred into eschatological hope. This kind of resurrection changes a selfish, individualistic, escapist anomie into a communal, united, realistic commitment to the common good. It becomes a struggle for a humane life and dignity for all the people. This resurrection prevents the people's bitter resentment and moral indignation from evaporating in self-hatred and converts it into a fierce demand for God's universal justice. If necessary, the people's enormous energy may also be directed to a decisive, organized explosion. This is a revolutionary religion. This miraculous conversion which conceived the mystery of revival may also bring a decisive spiritual revival. This conversion is the philosophy of *tan*, the determination to choose the circumstances of one's death, that my hero, Chang Il Tam, sings about.

Since my college years when I suffered from tuberculosis, I have passionately wanted to understand both my personal situation and my country's. How could I overcome my terror of death and how could South Korea find its way out of the ubiquitous spiritual dehumanization and material poverty? I heard something then about the Tong Hak teaching that "man is heaven." At first, it was a low murmuring that made only a slight impression. Later I learned more about the Tong Hak rebellion, and an image took shape in my mind. I could see that awesome band of starving peasants, their proud banner proclaiming "An end to violence, save the people! " as they marched off to fight. Suddenly that Tong Hak teaching became a loud cry as thunderous as the battle cries of those marching peasants.

I have been grappling with that image for ten years. At some point, I gave it a name: "The unity of God and revolution." I also changed the phrase "man is heaven" into "rice is heaven" and used it in my poetry.

That vague idea of "the unity of God and revolution" stayed with me as I continued my long arduous search for personal and political answers, and as I became very interested in contemporary Christian thought and activism. European social reformers, including Ernst Troeltsch, Frederic Ozanam, Karl Marx, and others had been absorbed into the grand edifice of Christian thought. Their ideas were now being re-examined and developed in new directions. I was intrigued by efforts to combine Marxist social reform and Christian beliefs as evinced in the 1972 Santiago Declaration of Christians for Socialism.

The synthesis draws from diverse sources. One example is the adaptation of the teachings of Marx and Jesus. Marx's contribution is his structural epistemology, which maintains that social oppression blocks human salvation. From Jesus' teachings we take his humanism, which advocates love for all people and human dignity, his emphasis on rebirth as the means to salvation, the idea of the God of hope who brings salvation, equality, and liberation on earth, and the activities of Jesus of Nazareth during his life.

The synthesis tries to unify and integrate these concepts. In my view this is not a mechanical process, a rote grafting of bits of Marxism onto Christianity. The union produces something entirely new. (The new synthesis is not finished. Its gestalt cannot be defined; it is still amorphous. Therefore I must decline to use the existing terminology. The Korean people are suffering from the tragic reality of a divided peninsula. This division has become the excuse for brutal repression: Everything is done in the name of "national security," the threat from the North. Under this police-state system South Korean society has become rigid, intolerant, frightened; our intellectual life is as airless and barren as the valleys of the moon. The authorities, who are hypersensitive and always suspicious of new and possibly "dangerous" thoughts, may attempt to label my ideas as a certain ideology; I reject this false labelling of an unfinished "product." I stand on my human right to be creative. Original ideas are not mass-produced on an assembly line.)

My image of the unity of God and revolution was clarified by Pope John XXIII's encyclical *Mater et Magistra:* "The mystery of Jesus and the loaves of bread is a temporal miracle which shows the future heaven." I also benefitted from the writings of the liberation theologians: Fredrick Herzog, James Cone, Richard Shaull, Paul Lehmann, Jürgen Moltmann, J.B. Metz, Tödt, Hugo Assmann, Reinhold Niebuhr, Dietrich Bonhöffer, and others. Papal statements after Vatican II as well as such encyclicals as *Rerum Novarum* and *Quadragesimo Anno* provided insights. The greatest single influence on my thinking, however, has been my participation since 1971 in the Korean Christian movement for human rights. This experience convinced me that the Korean tradition of resistance and revolution, with its unique vitality under the incredibly negative circumstances prevailing here, are precious materials for a new form of human liberation. This rich lode will be of special value to the Third World. Shaped and polished by the tools of liberation theology, our experience may inspire miraculous new forms of *Missio Dei* in the gritty struggle of the South Korean people.

My ballad *Chang Il Tam* attempts to express these ideas through the teachings and intellectual pilgrimage of one holy man who speaks in the form of gospels. However, the Park regime has seized my notes as proof of a "conspiracy to publish subversive materials."

Chang Il Tam is a thief, the son of a prostitute and a *paekchong* [an outcast strata that performs unclean tasks such as slaughtering animals, tanning, etc.]. A failure in life, despondent, Chang suddenly attains enlightenment and becomes a preacher of liberation. Chang emulates Im Kok Chong [Korea's legendary Robin Hood] in believing that the poor should "re-liberate" what the rich have stolen from them and divide it equally among the needy. He begins stealing from the rich and giving to the poor, is arrested and thrown into jail, whereupon he teaches the other prisoners about revolution. One day Chang is unfairly disciplined. Angrily throwing caution to the winds, he shouts "We must be liberated! Down with the hated bourgeoisie!" (My working notes cover only a portion of his proselytizing in prison; these are his early radical ideas. The government claims they are identical with *my* ideas and therefore constitute irrefutable proof that I am a Communist!)

Chang escapes from prison, is hunted by the police, and finally hides in a filthy back alley where some prostitutes are plying their trade. He calls to the prostitutes, "Oh, you are all my Mother!" He kisses their feet and declares: "The soles of your feet are heaven" and "God is in your decaying wombs" and "God's place is with the lowest of the low."

Chang later goes to live on Mt. Kyeryong and preaches about a paradise in the land of the Eastern Sea [Korea]. He teaches a systematic religious discipline in three stages: *Sich'onju*, acceptance of God and service to Him; *Yangch'onju*, cultivation of God in your heart and subordination of everything to God's will; and *Saengch'onju*. Chang preaches "communal ownership of property," teaches about revolution, stresses the unity of prayer and action, and advocates "resistance against the tide." His major ideas include "the transformation of the lowest into heaven," the traveller's path from this world to heaven as revolution, the need to purge the wild beasts that lurk within human hearts, symbolic of the *paekchong's* occupation, and the corruption of this world and the paradise of the Eastern Sea in the next.

Chang Il Tam preaches to the workers and farmers. He builds an altar in the wilderness, starts a huge bonfire, and casts everything old into the flames. He teaches the people that although violence is unavoidable, *tan* is desirable. Chang leads the multitude toward the evil palace in the capital, Seoul. The throng all carry beggars' cans. At this point Chang proclaims that paradise is "to share food with others" and that "food is heaven." They reach the capital where food is abundant and continue through the city on the eternal journey toward paradise where food is shared by all. (This journey implies an endless transmigratory discipline: to the destination and then a return to the place where there is no food.)

During the march to Seoul, Chang is defeated in a battle. The government offers a reward, and the traitor Judas turns Chang in. Chang remains silent, saying nothing in his own defense. He is convicted of violating the Anti-Communist Law and the National Security Law and of inciting rebel-

"He calls to the prostitutes, 'Oh, you are my Mother!' He kisses their feet and declares: 'The soles of your feet are heaven' and 'God is in your decaying wombs.' "

lion. Chang is taken out to be executed and just before he is beheaded breaks his silence and sings a song, "Food Is Heaven."

> Food is heaven
> You can't make it on your own
> Food should be shared
> Food is heaven.
>
> We all see
> The same stars in heaven
> How natural that we
> All share the same food.
>
> Food is heaven
> As we eat
> God enters us
> Food is heaven.
>
> Oh, food
> Should be shared and eaten by all.

Chang is resurrected three days later. His severed head seeks out the traitor Judas, decapitates him, and places itself on his trunk. The traitor's body is joined with the saint's destiny. This weird union of holiness, goodness, and truth, accomplished through Judas's wicked intelligence, is both Chang's revenge *and* salvation for the sinner. It expresses the manifold paradoxes of Chang's thought.

My tentative denouement for the ballad is, "The song 'Food Is Heaven' has become a raging storm sweeping into every corner of South Korea."

That is the general outline of the ballad. I repeat that Chang Il Tam's world is in flux. Religious ascetism and revolutionary action, the works of Jesus, the struggle of

Ch'oe Che U (founder of the Tong Hak) and Chon Pong Jun (commander of the Tong Hak peasant army), a yearning for the communal life of early Christianity, and a deep affection for the long, valiant resistance of the Korean people are all a part of Chang's kaleidoscopic world. So are Paulo Freire's *The Pedagogy of the Oppressed*, Frantz Fanon's ideas on violence, the direct action of Blanquism, the Christian view of humanity as flawed by original sin, the Catholic doctrine of the omnipresence of God and the Buddhist concept of the transmigration of the soul, the populist redistributive egalitarianism of Im Kok Chong and Hong Kil Tong, and Tong Hak teachings of *Sich'onju* and *Yangch'onju*. Some of these movements and doctrines combine and coalesce; others clash in mighty confrontation.

I have no intention of trying to provide a consistent theoretical elucidation of *Chang Il Tam* while I am still writing it. That is impossible; when the work is finished, I may be able to do so.

DID I VIOLATE THE ANTI-COMMUNIST LAW?

The charge that I am a Communist rests on three allegations. First, that my notebooks for *Chang Il Tam* and other works contain statements favorable to North Korea. Second, that my statements about the so-called People's Revolutionary Party (PRP) "praise, encourage, and support" a subversive organization. Third, that my possession of several books was beneficial to North Korea because they "praise, encourage, and support" subversive ideas.

National security laws have been misused in South Korea for many years. The constant, expedient, indiscriminate, and conspiratorial application of the dreaded Article Four of the Anti-Communist Law has been the most malevolent restriction on the intellectual and spiritual growth of the republic.[3] It has been used to deprive us of freedom of speech and to impose a suffocating culture of silence that has killed democracy and sustained a corrupt dictatorship. I oppose the misuse of Article Four with every ounce of strength in my body. It is repugnant to everything I believe in and stand for. I call on others to oppose the regime's attempt to gag me with this filthy rag of a law. We must have freedom of thought and expression. Individuality—conscience and creativity—must be protected.

I shall discuss the state's allegations one by one. I was harassed by the KCIA interrogators to admit that some of my notes for *Chang Il Tam* were based on Mao Tse-tung's thought. As I stated above, the work draws on the seminal ideas, theories, and accomplishments of world civilization. Mao's *On Contradiction* is an important contribution to political theory. But the KCIA were so proud of themselves! At last they had found a real "communist" connection. They said I was a Maoist who joined the Catholic church because I followed Mao's teaching on the transformation and unity of antagonisms. My notes included the words, "God and revolution, bread and freedom, the unity of heaven and earth"—all phrases that correspond to the resolution of contradictions. To my astonishment, the KCIA even attributed my use of the word "resurrection" to Mao! They said the "resolution" of death into resurrection was the resolution of contradiction! Even perverse sophistry has its limits, one would think. Perhaps under the circumstances I can be excused for not admiring the vivid imagination and creativity of the prosecutor.

The police of the Republic of Korea are not much for subtle distinctions. They regard materialism as identical with metaphysics. At the faintest whiff of dialectics, they stick the communist label on you. In South Korea, Lao Tzu, Confucius, Jesus, the Buddha, anybody and everybody concerned with fundamental truth or essential reality would be a Communist.

I said above that it would be premature to categorize *Chang Il Tam*. But I *can* say that it is not socialist realism, a vehicle for Marxist ideas. The work is apocalyptical, prophetic, full of allegory, mystery, and symbolism. I use supernatural occurrences and the fanciful events conjured up by the sensitivity and imagination of peasants and workers. I dab in a touch of the abstract with bizarre illusions. I use death, chaos, insecurity, terror, revolution, despair, melancholy, atrocities, executions, and decadence to create the overall tone. I attempt to describe a ghastly, blood-soaked, transitional period by the use of furious language and violent incidents. My work bears no resemblance to the pallid tone, naturalistic descriptions, and realistic plots of conventional socialist writing. There are no romances between steel workers and their blast furnaces in *Chang Il Tam*.

That is what I am working on. It is far from finished. Nevertheless, the government says it was written "to aid the Northern puppet regime." What can I say? There has been much publicity recently about the government's "Five Year Plan to Encourage Literature." But what they are doing to me is how they really "encourage" literature.

Let's look at the second allegation. I had notes for a play called *Maltuk* about a day laborer by that name who fights against the bourgeoisie. The police and KCIA insist that this is a Marxist writing which calls for the overthrow of the bourgeoisie by workers and peasants. They are so eager to find Communists that they react like Pavlov's dog to the word "bourgeoisie" and neurotically reach for the Anti-Communist Law. Just because Marx called a flower a flower, am I supposed to call it something else? The word "bourgeoisie" is an internationally accepted historical term. If the mere use of the word or the expression of contempt for something "bourgeois" proves a person is a Communist, where does that leave the French Catholic George Bernanos, who said, "I hate the bourgeoisie"? One hardly need cite foreign examples. Don't we hear the word everyday as a half humorous term for the rich? That is how I used it. To be more exact, my use of the word "bourgeoisie" has the limited meaning of the "corrupt ruling elite" who dominate South Korea. They are synonymous with the "Five Bandits."

Maltuk is based on the rebellious servant character in traditional mask dramas. The plot evolves from a popular protest against corruption and privilege. The protagonist is a laborer, but he is not trying to start a revolution to impose a dictatorship of the proletariat. I am trying to portray a rebel from the lower stratum of society, far lower than organized industrial workers, in fact. My idea was to make my hero a "debased *ch'onmin*," a stratum shunned by society as subhuman. He is a typical dehumanized South Korean, spiritually and physically robbed of his personhood. I want to describe his despair and the divine inspiration that rescues him. I will show the "reciprocal effect of action and prayer" which leads him to resist and regain his human dignity. I placed this interaction in Maltuk, a "rebellious, sweaty, dirty South Korean peasant" and stressed hope. I tried to describe a certain world of "community" which appears in the resultant eschatological vision. This is also a visionary manifestation of an oppression-free society, the eternal theme of true art. The drama is sustained by an imagination rooted in Christian eschatology; it is not derived from any political ideology. The allegation that it "was written to aid the Northern puppets" couldn't be more preposterous.

I want to explain why I wrote *Five Bandits*, *Groundless Rumors*, *Chang Il Tam*, *Maltuk*, and other works. So they could be used by someone? No. Because *I* wanted to write them. I had no choice. They were deep inside me, stirring, swirling. I had to let them burst out. I wrote because I had to. That was the only reason.

Next, the "People's Revolutionary Party" matter. I wrote about the torture of Ha Chae Wan and I held a press conference to ask for the release of the "PRP" prisoners. The government terms these actions as "support for the propaganda activities of the Northern puppets" that "benefited the People's Revolutionary Party, a subversive organization."

For the sake of argument, let's say that my statement about the torture of the "PRP" prisoners was identical with the North Korean "propaganda" on the case. The question really is, Did I "support" their version or did they "support" mine? They did not meet Ha Chae Wan. *I* met him and I heard his story directly from him. I just told the world what I heard. I did not say Ha Chae Wan was tortured on the basis of a North Korean broadcast. Does similarity of content mean "support"? If it does, thousands of ordinary citizens, intellectuals, religious leaders, students, and politicians who demanded the "release of the democratic leaders" arrested in 1974 must be pro-Communist sympathizers, since the North certainly must have advocated the same thing. Don't they all have to be charged under the Anti-Communist Law? Hasn't this nonsense gone too far?

Did I speak out to help the "People's Revolutionary Party, a subversive organization"? How could that possibly have been my reason? I knew certain facts that every person in this country needed to know. I made those horrible facts public in the interests of civil rights and democracy in South Korea. Consider my position. I had no connection with the "PRP" and I did not even know the prisoners. I was aware of course that the Park regime would retaliate against me. Why should I go so far just to help a subversive organization? Didn't I have anything better to do? The government as usual has a ready explanation. They say I called the PRP case a "fabrication" to conceal my own "communist sympathies"! Unless my memory is wrong, even the Prime Minister is supposed to have said in the National Assembly, "Kim Chi Ha is not a Communist." The KCIA assertion that I was trying to hide my "pro-communist sympathies" is absurdly illogical. Claiming the government had trumped-up charges against the "PRP" men would obviously bring me under suspicion.

I know the "PRP" men were tortured. What is the KCIA anyway? We all know they have tortured students and opposition party National Assembly members. Recently the National Assembly floor leader of the ruling Democratic Republican Party revealed that he also had been tortured by the KCIA. That is how they function; brutality and terror are their standard operating procedure. Anyone who thinks the "PRP" prisoners, who were being set up as Communists for execution, were not tortured ought to have their head examined. I spoke only about facts I had heard with my own ears and saw with my own eyes, facts I am absolutely certain of.

Was the "PRP" a subversive organization? Was there really a "PRP"? My suspicions have not been resolved by the Park regime's pronouncements. If the Park regime wants me to accept its version and to convince the public that I was wrong, they should bring back to life the eight men executed on April 9. Or perhaps they can call the ghosts of Ha Chae Wan and Yi Su Byong to testify on the state's behalf. I want to challenge the legality of these "PRP"-related charges.

Finally, we come to the most absurd items in the indictment, that some of the books in my storage shed were a threat to the state. The magazines *Hanyang* and *Chongmaek* I read in 1964. Mao's *On Practice* and *On Contradiction* I read in about 1969. I read those books and put them away years ago. How did these volumes gathering dust in my shed help North Korea?

TO ALL PEOPLE WHO LOVE FREEDOM AND JUSTICE

I believe that all who oppose repression and dictatorship and defend freedom, justice, and the rights of conscience still remain committed to the struggle against the corrupt Park regime. When I was released from prison on February 15, I reconfirmed my vow to resist this dictatorship as long as I live. I have explained in this statement the spurious charges against me. All those who know me will disregard any kind of slander against me at variance with this statement. Your understanding comforts me.

My prison notebooks contain ample proof that this statement is true. Furthermore, prison was not easy for me. But I gained precious experiences and inspiration through my fellowship with the other prisoners, supposedly the dregs of our society. The notebooks are not just about me; the truth of this period of our history is also there. I hope you can prevent their destruction.

Why have we been fighting against the Park regime? For human liberation. To recover the humanity God gave us, to be free people. Nothing is more important. We must press ahead. We will not be stopped. We shall overcome.

The government constantly asserts that the threat from North Korea is so serious that civil rights are an unpermissible luxury. But a corrupt, immoral dictatorship is the greatest spur to communism. What better argument do the Communists have than the Park regime? Dictatorial rule will never make South Korea secure. A country is strong and viable only when its democracy and freedom are protected and tyranny and oppression destroyed.

If we have no basic rights or representative government, what is there for us to defend? Our hopeless privation and disease, our endless despair and humiliation? Are we to risk our lives for these? In every neighborhood and village we must shout our opposition to this wretchedness.

We are not alone in this struggle. Men and women all over the world concerned with freedom will generously support our struggle. Our age demands truth and the passion to endure the suffering necessary to learn the truth.

We want to be free. To taste, feel, and transmit to our

children the freedom so long promised in South Korea. We must commit everything we are and hope to be to this noble cause. My prayers are with all of you in this courageous struggle.

POSTSCRIPT

Just before I was arrested in March the authorities searched my country house and the home where my son was staying. They seized four or five of my private notebooks. At first I wasn't sure what they were after, but the interrogator's questions provided a clue. They asked, "Weren't you asked to write a poem about the Kim Dae Jung kidnapping?" and "Where is that manuscript?"

I am not allowed to receive visitors or mail, to write anything, or even read the Bible. I cannot move around very much. This gloomy, cramped cell is a bit less than seven feet by seven.

I sit here in the dark angrily thinking about the uncertain future. But prison has not dimmed my spirits. These miserable conditions and the endless waiting have made me more determined than ever.

I feel a quiet composure, almost serenity. But I am terribly worried about what may happen to the individuals involved in making this statement public. My friends, please help these good people.

Do not grieve for me.

We will surely see each other again soon.

—Translated by the Japanese Commission for Justice and Peace

NOTES

1. Kim's forced "confession" states: "After advancing to college, I felt frustration and an inferiority complex since I could not enjoy a normal campus life, compared with other students, due to sickness and family hardship. These feelings developed into a sense of resistance against our social system. . . . Through my readings on communism, I have come to the conclusion that all irregularities and contradictions in our society derive from the capitalistic system and the means to root out such irregularities is to overthrow the existing system through a proletarian revolution in compliance with the teachings of Marx" ("The Case Against Kim Chi Ha, The True Identity of the Poet," p. 11; this pamphlet, distributed by the KCIA, includes Kim's confession, excerpts from his prison notes, lists of books seized at his home, etc.).

2. The Tong Hak (Eastern Learning) religion was founded by Ch'oe Che U in the 1860s. It combined elements of Confucianism, Buddhism, indigenous beliefs, Christianity, and nationalism. Local revolts by Tong Hak followers in 1892 spread to a major uprising, the Tong Hak Rebellion, in 1893–94.

3. Article Four of the Anti-Communist Law states:

"1. Any person who has benefited the anti-State organization by praising, encouraging, or siding with, or through other means, the activities of an anti-State organization or their components or the communist organizations outside the Republic of Korea shall be punished by imprisonment at hard labor for not more than seven years.

"2. The same penalty shall apply to any person who has, for the purpose of committing the acts as provided for in the foregoing paragraph, produced, imported, duplicated, kept in custody, transported, disseminated, sold or acquired documents, drawings, and any other similar means of expression" ("The Case Against Kim Chi Ha," pp. 44–45).

Letter to the National Priests Association for the Realization of Justice

(The following letter, dated May 14, 1975, was attached to the Declaration of Conscience; like the Declaration it was smuggled out of Kim Chi Ha's prison cell and then out of the country.)

Praise to the Lord!

How are you all? Thanks to the Lord's mercy and your prayers, I am fine.

I am in solitary confinement in a dark cell and forbidden to write or read, even Scripture. I spend each day in meditation, surrounded by these gloomy walls. Nonetheless, my spirits are closer to the Lord than ever before. Not a single ray of sunlight reaches me now but I cannot forget those brighter days when your powerful cries for justice and mercy shook the citadel of this tyranny we live under. Buoyed by your call for freedom, my soul has repeatedly burst out of my cell and over the high prison walls to be with you in the desperate struggle. As long as the Lord is at my side and you continue your dauntless movement out there, I have no misgivings about this tribulation the Lord has presented me as a sign of his divine will. I only hope I am devout enough to persevere in adversity and attain spiritual renewal. But I have been anxious recently and I decided to write this letter.

According to my lawyers, some of you have believed the

"I am in solitary
confinement in a dark cell
and forbidden to write
or read, even Scripture.
I spend each day
in meditation, surrounded
by these gloomy walls.
Nonetheless, my spirits
are closer to the Lord
than ever before."

government's vile charge that I am a Communist and are having doubts about me.

I am not a Communist. My opposition to oppression and exploitation and my hopes for revolution aren't because I am a Communist but because I am a radical Catholic. I realize that I may be misunderstood but I am not afraid of that. I am far more concerned that this government conspiracy may eventually lead to suppression of your activities. This is what has been troubling me.

As you know, the authorities are trying to fabricate a case against me by alleging that I am a Communist who infiltrated the Catholic church. They call me a treacherous, cunning communist agent, pretending to be a democrat. One can easily imagine that the real target of this nefarious attack is your Association and the activities of all democratic elements, including both the Catholic and Protestant churches, to restore democracy in South Korea. The government's objective apparently is to charge the entire democratic movement, including the students, with being "pro-Communist" and launch a new, sweeping wave of repression.

Perhaps it is presumptuous for me to say this, but now is the time when you must be most determined and resolute. I can wish for nothing more than that your passion for bearing this cross will become even stronger.

The church is a beacon in the stormy, dangerous waters. It lights the way to shore. Thus the people, foundering in agony, look up to the church with such respect.

The Association's activities are especially a symbol of hope not only for the future of Korea but also for the people of the Third World.

This responsibility is a great honor for Koreans and also a burden, a painful duty. If it is God's will, no matter how heavy the burden we have no choice but to accept it. You priests have already joyously accepted this grave responsibility. The heavier the burden the more magnificent will be the Lord's will, your conduct, and relationship between your actions and the people's salvation. The greater the duty and the more onerous the task, the greater will be the respect and trust afforded to the holy church by the afflicted people.

You priests bear this responsibility. To work for both the restoration of democracy and the people's material welfare is to tread a perilous path indeed. However, this very difficulty distinguishes the Association from ordinary political activities. I believe that your activities constitute a collective, prayerful, ascetic bearing of the cross, and a pilgrimage to heaven.

No matter how important national security may be regarded, it cannot take precedence over the Lord's command for human revival. Even granting the importance of national security, only the unity of the people assures it. And democracy is a prerequisite for unity. That is precisely why the movement to restore democracy is the most compelling task before the people and our church.

There is no other way to achieve national unity than for the regime to acknowledge its responsibility for the disasters it has brought upon the republic and to resign. Please do not be misled by the government's sophisticated duplicity. Let God's word ring out and shatter this oppressive silence.

The Association is the only hope of salvation. Please light the way for me, a humble servant of the Lord, and for the brethren. Please, with the help of God's limitless power, make your actions the salvation and joy of our people now so overwhelmed with hunger and sorrow.

I firmly believe that the Lord gives nothing to those who seek indolence but to those who seek righteousness all things shall be given.

God bless you.

—*Translated by the Japanese Commission for Justice and Peace*

Court Interrogation

June 1976 (Excerpts)

(The following excerpts from Kim Chi Ha's testimony in court have been reconstructed from reports by eyewitnesses.)

Kim Chi Ha: There are some things I wish to make clear in this court. Due to the strenuous examination of the Central Intelligence Agency (KCIA) and the prosecuting authorities, I am in a state of extreme physical weakness and mental confusion, and as a result of duress and exhaustion I have "confessed" to many things that are not true. Consequently, the only place in which I can make the facts clear is this court.

Also, ever since I was taken into custody last year my rights as a human being have been totally disregarded; there has been a ban on reading matter, interviews, movement, and correspondence. A further instance of this trampling on my rights is that it was necessary to send a "Declaration of Conscience" to the church refuting a so-called confession, which I was forced to make, to being a Communist who had infiltrated the Catholic church. They have subsequently pressurized me into another such "confession," and since August last year I have been subjected to extreme psychological tortures such as solitary confinement. I am not really in a free condition, and I lack the confidence to express myself in a simple summary statement.

As a result, (1) I would like a guarantee of complete freedom to make a statement. (2) Since my memory is not clear in regard to the materials of evidence, while the court is examining this material I would like to be granted the opportunity to have it in writing before me. (3) I would like you to use your influence to insure that this disregard for human rights, which is actually a retaliation by the government against me, does not occur again.

Chief Prosecutor: At present, as far as this case is concerned, the defendant is not undergoing the trial under duress. As a result, the court is unable to grant the requested reform measures. We have no way of knowing about the defendant's treatment.

Question (hereafter Q): When you were at the university is it not true that you received copies of *Das Kapital*, *The Communist Manifesto*, Lenin's *State and Revolution* and *Theory of Imperialism*, Freuds's *Art and Society*, and Lukác's *History and Class Consciousness* from Kim Jung Tae and read them?

Answer (hereafter A): False. That is contrary to the facts. It is true that I received one copy each of *Das Kapital* and *The Anti-Dühring Theory* from Kim Jung Tae and read them, and also I borrowed the German editions of *Art and Society* and *History and Class Consciousness* from the Seoul University Library and read them. I have not read the *Communist Manifesto* or the two books by Lenin.

This is simply the contents of an announcement released by the Central Intelligence Agency in which they forced me to say that I had read the books on a list which they had prepared.

Q: From February 1967, when you entered Seoul City Hospital for treatment of tuberculosis, until May of that year it is said that you listened to a radio program dealing with Marxist and Leninist theory broadcast from the North every day at five o'clock as a means of theoretical armament.

A: No, that is not true. It is completely contrary to the facts. At that time of day, since I had time on my hands, I listened to drama and song programs, and I occasionally twirled the dial and perhaps five or six times got a broadcast from Pyongyang; it was completely by chance that I happened to hear it. The so-called theoretical armament is an unfounded charge unworthy of mention. What kind of "theoretical armament" would a person weak in body and spirit be able to talk about? It's a fabrication by the Central Intelligence Agency.

Q: In your memorandum on *Maltuk* it says, "The coercion, exploitation, oppression, and deception of the bourgeois present the classic contents of tragedy, and in their driving of the people to the last strand of hair and sucking of the people to the last drop of blood a positively vampiric scene is depicted." Is this not the attack of a Communist on the capitalists?

A: No. This is simply an attempt to expose and attack the existing corrupt dictatorship with expressions that find their basis in Christian social ethics. Expressions of this type can be found in many places in the Old Testament, such as Amos, chapters 6 and 8, Isaiah 3 and 5, Micah, 2, 3, and 6. For example, in Micah 3 it says, "You have flayed the skin of my people and torn the meat from their bones and eaten it, and you have taken the remaining skin and bones and put them in pots and ovens and used it as meat." Attacks as severe as this can be found in many places. Compared to them mine is not much to speak of. As far as Christian radicalism is concerned it's a very natural expression.

Q: You write, "The central aspects of the anatomy of exploitation." Isn't the term "exploitation" used here a communist concept?

A: Already in Exodus 22 and Leviticus 19 and 25, God prohibited exploitation and set forth a severe punishment for it. In addition, all the prophets criticized exploitation. The

German theologian Gunther Bornkamm in his book *Jesus of Nazareth* defined exploitation as the social original sin. It is the duty of the Christian to oppose exploitation and to attack it.

Q: In *Maltuk* do you not treat the problem of exploitation as the most basic and essential problem?

A: No. The various aspects of moral decline such as oppression, coercion, exploitation, deception, sexual prodigality comprised a list. Exploitation was only one item in that list.

Q: It is said that in October of 1973 you had occasion to meet Bishop Daniel Chi of Wonju parish.

A: That is correct. I inquired of Bishop Chi about present movements and developments in the Catholic church, especially those after the Second Vatican Council. I also inquired about the love of Jesus and the love of one's neighbor, also about the unification of social revolution and liberation of the soul, in other words, the mystery of the cross, and whether this was the central point of Catholic teaching. Upon borrowing and reading a copy of John XXIII's encyclical *Mater et Magistra* I discovered that the principle I had searched for was found in Catholicism and I became a convert.

Q: Is it true that you were interested in a Chinese type of revolution, which found its basis in the particularly Asian quality of Mao Tse-tung?

A: This is a delicate question so it requires a rather lengthy explanation. It is true that I found in Catholicism the principle of hope I had sought for. The truth of Catholicism is universal and humanitarian, but in order for it to be successfully applied and put into action in the particularly complex situation in our country, it is necessary to overcome such methodological problems as how to establish it, how to spread it among the people, and how to organize it. In order to solve these problems, I thought it would be necessary to look at examples from our own social history, involving particular situations and traditions of social movements such as the Tong Hak Movement for Equity and Im Kok Chung. I also thought it would be necessary to study the experience of social movements in other countries, in particular how the thinking of the West came to be developed in various continents, for example, by Frantz Fanon in Africa, Paulo Freire in South America, Gandhi in India, and Mao Tse-tung in China. I wanted to read about them extensively and compare them. Mao Tse-tung's ideas were merely one part of a spectrum of ideas I was interested in methodologically.

Q: In the period of direct interrogation the defendant said that the present government is pro-Japanese. What are the defendants views on this pro-Japanese issue?

A: I participated in the protest against the 1964 and 1965 Korea-Japan conferences. At the time, all the people expressed a deep anxiety about the results of those conferences. But the worries of the people were not without foundation. The inroads of Japanese pro-colonialist education, political interference, the trend of servility to Japanese education, the worsening of the situation of dependence on Japan, Japan's hateful superior attitude, and Korea's attitude of inferiority and feelings of inequality were getting progressively worse. This was, in effect, a piling on top of the past relations of the two countries, an enmity relationship that invited danger. These matters relate on all points to the future of Japan and Korea. The southeast coast of Korea is being taken over as an industrial area for the industries of western Japan. By the introduction of polluting industries large scale profits have been extracted. The Korean government is taking measures to legally insure the continuation of those profits. At present, the exploitation of Korean labor with Japanese capital presents a new problem. The Korean government is endangering the fate of democracy in Korea to an extreme degree.

To prevent further tragedies in the future, there is no other path except for the people of the two countries to join together in a mutual struggle. But in a struggle like this it won't do for the Japanese people to assume an attitude of superiority, or for the Korean people to feel inferior or take a position based on the concept of their worthlessness as a people. As far as the Korean problem is concerned, the Japanese side will, on the contrary, have to begin with a movement toward repentance, starting with a spirit of denial of the spirit of nationalism. And the Korean side must begin with a movement toward self-awakening, beginning with a strong affirmation of themselves as a people. Those in high places must lower themselves and the low raise themselves up accordingly. Having this principle as a basis, the mutual struggle can become a movement of true friendship between the two countries.

Q: Could you please express your views concerning present government policies?

A: It is my conviction that the sooner the present policies are done away with the better it will be for the country. The present condition is one where the existing policies have done away with democracy and robbed the people of their basic rights, including the right to a livelihood. Those in power have pressed the people into a hopelessly gray existence. The present government is a tyrannical group of oppressors that has deprived the people of their lives and damaged the common good. Since this group of oppressors is in direct opposition to God's justice, it is natural that we should do away with them. If the present government does not step down by itself, I believe it is the justice of God for the people to take steps to remove it.

Q: Have you participated in the activities of your university circles?

A: I didn't participate in the circles related to social science or politics. I was active in circles studying literature, drama, and the traditional arts. To give some examples, the Cinema Club, the Drama Group, the Literature Organization, the Uli Cultural Studies Group, and the Pansori and Talchim Research Organizations.

Q: Didn't you have a leadership role in the protest demonstrations against the Korea-Japan Conferences?

A: I myself thought that I was one of the leaders but I was treated by the police as just another blind follower.

Q: During your student days, if you had any particular spiritual system of ideals or system on which your activities were based, what were they?

A: In a word, I could say they were liberal. I hate to stick things within the confines of a certain defined framework. Lao Tzu says that if we say the Way is the Way it is already not the Way. I possessed a rather stubborn nature; in the process of seeking the true pearl of what I am I refused to make a definition of what I am. In other words, I had the idea that if I was able to get even the outline of that true pearl by the time I died, I would be happy.

Q: It is said that at the time you were in the hospital for treatment of tuberculosis you listened to the broadcast from the North and read Catholic pamphlets and felt intense perplexity and agonized over the problems between the two.

A: According to the doctor's diagnosis at that time, if I had entered the hospital one week later I would have been dead. I was suffering from severe breathing blockage and coughing up blood. What I read or heard, under those conditions, would hardly have made much sense. To suffer perplexity and agonize over a problem it is necessary for the love toward it to deepen. If a man encounters two completely unknown girls in the street, does he agonize over which one he should choose and which one he should reject? At the time I was unversed in both subjects and was unable to know about them in detail.

Q: What relation does literature have to a criticism of the present situation?

A: In the Bible, from Genesis onward, hidden subtle truths are revealed by means of allegory, satire, methods of comparison, and verbal violence. In other words, by these methods, dark matters are brought out into the light. I think it is the most important task of literature to bring hidden things out into the light. The contradictions, darkness, injustice, oppression, and exploitation that are hidden are brought forth and revealed.

Q: What were your motives for becoming a Catholic?

A: I was searching for a principle that offered, at the same time and by the same system, a unified solution to both the problem of our spiritual soul and the problem or our material existence. I happened to meet Bishop Chi and received his instruction. Upon finding such a principle in Catholic teachings I became a convert.

Q: What is the relation between Christianity and your opposition to oppression and tyranny?

A: Christianity is a religion that is opposed in principle to oppression and exploitation. Throughout the Old Testament there are passages that rebuke severely oppression and exploitation. In Isaiah 58 it says that to oppose oppression and exploitation and to put complete love for your neighbors into practice is the fundamental law of God. In Isaiah 11, it says that the place where there is no oppression or exploitation and no weeping or crying, where the cow lies down with the wolf and the badger with the lamb, in that place is the New Land, the New World.

In such writings as John XXIII's *Mater et Magistra* and *Pacem in Terris* and in the writings coming out of the Second Vatican Council, it is repeatedly defined that it is the duty of the Christian of today to oppose oppression and exploitation.

Q: You say you approve of revolution, but aren't there some differences between Christianity and revolutionary ideologies?

A: I believe in a wide sense that Christianity is a revolutionary religion. Christianity is shown to be a revolutionary religion in such passages as Matthew 25 and Luke 1. In other words, the principles whereby authoritarians, exploiters, and the high and mighty are brought down and chased out with open hands and the lowly, oppressed, and the poor are admitted, set free, and satisfied, are found in the Bible. These principles definitely explain revolution. But these principles are by no means limited to overcoming tyrannical oppression. That is a narrow meaning and refers only to the moment. In a broader sense, a Christian revolution is the apocalyptic vision of the mass resurrection of the people. Through a lasting collective struggle combined with prayer, it promises establishment of hope for the repentant and the practice of communal love. In the Old Testament, Yahweh interrupts the course of history and destroys injustice and through the voices of the prophets endlessly shows the way toward justice and peace. Through group movements God does away with exploitation and injustice and authoritarianism and frees those subjected to slavery. By these revolutions, battles, destructions, constructions, and through the constant testing and training of people, dynamic feats are accomplished. We can interpret this as the revolutionary history of Yahweh in the Old Testament.

To exhibit these revolutionary principles in the midst of the present political situation is the highest Christian action and it is the basic objective of revolutionary theology. The revolutionary gospel of Christianity demands that we take a stance transcending all wordly revolutionary ideologies. The Open Message to the Peoples of the Third World from Third World bishops said, "No, it is not God's will that a few rich people enjoy the goods of this world and exploit the poor. No, it is not God's will that some people remain poor and abject forever. No, religion is not the opiate of the people; it is a force that exalts the lowly and casts down the proud, that feeds the hungry and sends the sated away empty." But it also says that this stands in a position that transcends all ideologies.

In John 17 there is a prayer beseeching deliverance from evil. Father Camilo Torres interpreted this as the struggle against present evil, in other words revolution. The revolution mentioned here has no relation to socialistic revolutionary ideology and transcends it. Jesus was one who revealed an eternal revolution transcending class and ideology.

Q: What is a Catholic radical?

A: A Catholic radical has an attitude of complete self-sacrifice and untiring devotion toward the achievement of justice and truth. In the Bible there is the passage, "You should love the Lord your God with your whole heart, your whole strength, your whole will and you should love your neighbor as yourself." To fulfill this command one undergoes any kind of sacrifice unquestioningly with tireless self-denial and complete dedication, risking death or imprisonment and, should circumstances demand it, taking up the cross and following Christ. Archbishop Camara, Bishop Chi, and many others, not to mention Jesus Christ himself, are all classic examples of Catholic radicals.

Q: What are the conceptions and motives in *Chang Il Tam* and *Maltuk?*

A: During my imprisonment at a corrective institution I observed that the outrage of the lowest classes was incredibly intense, and I began to develop the theory that perhaps this energy could be channeled into something socially constructive. I was impressed by the purity of their passion and spirit and I began to hold the conviction that a Messiah would arise from these lowest classes.

Q: Are the sections on *Chang Il Tam* and *Maltuk* the only things contained in your memorandums?

A: No. There are conceptions stemming from different periods. My thinking system is such that I have conceptions for seven or eight and sometimes as many as fifteen works at the same time. If you want to call it a strange system of thinking then I guess it is. My memory of the contents of the memorandums is not exact, but I think in those four or five notebooks there are plans for about thirty to forty different works.

Q: Do the expressions used in the memorandums have any relation to verbal violence?

A: Yes. Jesus used verbal violence on many occasions to bring about repentance, for example, in the passage, "You brood of vipers, I have come to give light to the world, I come bringing not peace, but the sword." It is using violent language within a controlled scope to deliver an indignant and angry blow to the consciousness of a people oppressed by authority and in a state of near-mesmerization, and thus bring about an awakening to liberation and a sense of one's own worth.

Q: What is the Christian position on the "bourgeois?"

A: "It is as difficult for the rich to enter heaven as it is for a camel to pass through the eye of a needle." Also in the

Gospel of Matthew: "You cannot serve God and riches at the same time." That explains the position.

Q: What was the reason that you had special interest in Mao Tse-tung around 1969?

A: From around the end of 1968 the newspapers were full of articles pertaining to the Great Cultural Revolution in Communist China. Mao was often quoted. Among the quotations was the passage, "We must wipe away the 'I' or 'Ego' from the individual consciousness as a concept concerning the self." This and others like it had an almost religious dimension to them. Thus I became more or less interested in the Cultural Revolution and Mao Tse-tung.

Q: What was the central focus of your interest in Mao Tse-tung?

A: I was not interested in Mao's Marxist-Leninist philosophical principles. I was interested in the creative power whereby he proposed to develop those principles under conditions such as China's with its long traditions and a society composed of so many millions. At the time, China had had a history of the rapacity of colonialism, the remnants of feudalism, the troubles of internal war, Japanese invasion, and fierce competitiveness.

Q: The situations in Mao's China and in Korea are different. Despite such differences, do you think that it is possible to put Maoist principles into practice in Korea?

A: I think it is completely impossible. Even if we say that they are truths, it is impossible to overlook the particular circumstances of time and the differences between the two peoples.

Q: What was your reason for selecting such figures as "Chang Il Tam" and "Maltuk" to appear as the heroes of the urban poor?

A: It is true that I have made the urban poor the heroes of my works. The "vanguard" in the *Five Bandits* leave the countryside and because of hunger steal and eat the bread.

Chang Il Tam is a thief. Maltuk is a day laborer and a classic example of the untouchable lower class. Making these urban poor the heroes of my works, I make a direct connection with Christian salvation thought. The first objective of Christ's salvation were Samaritans and the sick, mentally ill, blind, lame, prostitutes, orphans, and day laborers who were treated almost as offenders. Likewise, in the Gospels of Matthew and Luke there is the idea that Christ came to save not the righteous, but the offenders. Also it says that the tax-collectors and prostitutes will be admitted into heaven first. This kind of thinking also appears in Corinthians 1, and in the Gospel of John, chapter 11.

In the materials coming out of the Second Vatican Council there is a section that deals with the arts. There it is stated expressly that, in order to bring God's salvation and the glory of Christ into our lives, it is necessary to express strongly the true state of darkness, pain, and tragedy that exist in the world.* This type of idea comes forth in the works of the English Catholic novelist Graham Greene and in the works of the French painter Rouault. I cannot help but think that the message of rebirth for humanity found in the Gospels must be made known and propagated among those poor who are presently in "prison." In other words, the idea that the most extreme tragedy can change into the most extreme glory of God takes the form of a paradox. I have come to think that in the midst of this the true light of Christ can begin to shine. I think that the first target of the plan of salvation must be these tragic poor. By making the poor the heroes of my works and having them gain victory, I was trying to express the possibility of salvation.

*"Decree on the Instruments of Social Communication," no. 7.

Q: What is the relationship between the *lumpenproletariat* and the Democratic People's Revolution?

A: Our country obviously belongs to the Third World. It has all the characteristics of a Third World society: chronic poverty, the high-handedness of dictatorial powers, intervention from outside, the remnants of feudalism, and other conditions related with these in a complex fashion. On the other hand, it also contains some of the characteristics of a rich society found in the advanced societies: luxury, pleasure-seeking, corruption, an almost schizophrenic level of division, and a rampage of commercial messages. This is not just in the cities, but has spread to the countryside.

In the midst of such conditions, what is the direction of a Democratic People's Revolution? Frantz Fanon said that the leader of the struggle for democracy and social revolution in the backward countries must come forth from the "wretched of the earth." Herbert Marcuse believes the possibility lies in those who are both spiritually and materially trampled on and reviled to the point of their very souls. As a matter of fact, the particular characteristic of the present situation is that a spiritual as well as a material solution is called for, not just for the backward countries, but for the whole world, rich and poor. In other words, the world as a whole is showing gradually signs that both God and revolution will be necessary.

I participated in the April 19th and June 3rd movements. The ones who persisted to the end were not the students and the factory workers; rather it was the shoeshine boys, the chewing-gum vendors, newspaper hawkers, prostitutes, the jobless, porters and day laborers. I think that one reason that the April 19th movement failed as a democratic revolution was that we forgot about the blood of these people. I believe therefore that we must place the poor in the center of the movement and have them assume a role directly connected with a People's Democratic Revolution with our sympathy and support.

Q: Could you relate traditional Catholic social principles, liberation theology, and their adoption and adaptation in this country?

A: The relationship between the three is so deep that it is impossible to separate them. I will use an analogy to explain the relationship between the Gospels and the papal encyclicals, the relation of the church and liberation and revolutionary theologies, and finally their establishment in a united society. The Gospels and the papal encyclicals, because of their universal scope, can be compared to the base of the fan. The form taken by the process of adapting these universal truths to the particular historical and social conditions of a country can be compared to the framework of the fan. The base of the fan is one unit; but the framework of the fan is comprised of many sections that are the varying forms adaptation takes, depending on the individual conditions of each situation. The fact that the base of the fan is a single unit means that there is one fundamental principle. Liberation theology and revolutionary theology can be compared to the paper that combines the main truths, which are the base of the fan, and the individual societal conditions, which comprise the framework of the fan. Revolutionary theology and liberation theology are the spirit of the age. With the combination of these three elements the wind of a Christian revolution begins to blow.

Q: Could it be said that works of the defendant such as *Five Bandits*, *Maltuk*, *Groundless Rumors*, and *Chang Il Tam* benefit and sympathize with the North?

A: Would any self-respecting author write words that benefited the North? The works themselves express the reasons they were written. As long as the North is in existence is it impossible to criticize the absurdities and contradictions taking place here? Aren't the ones who are producing these absurdities and contradictions benefiting the North much more?

Q: As a writer and a poet what are your views concerning freedom of expression?

A: Freedom of expression means freedom of speech or words. This is a basic tenet of democracy. The history of democracy is a history of the struggle for freedom of expression. The "culture of silence," a term widely used in the Third World, refers to the gloomy conditions whereby those in power, the dictators, exploiters, and oppressors, cover the truth from the eyes of the people and paralyze any human thought or judgment. It is the essence of democracy to fight against such a "culture of silence." Freedom of expression and freedom of speech are weapons to be used to tear open the enclosing net of the dictatorial power's "culture of silence."

Silence and speech are in opposition. Speech is that which rescues the truth from darkness. But silence is the evil power that throws the truth into darkness. The expression, "the Word was God," means that God himself is speech.

Freedom of expression is the most important tenet of democracy. In the case of liberating oppressed people and restoring them to human dignity it provides the life-line. If we obstruct this, then people will be left with only the cries of animals.

They will be able only to writhe in agony. Writhing in agony is a violent action. But Christianity is against bloodshed. Thus freedom of speech and freedom of expression are the last stronghold, if people are going to live human lives.

Final Statement in Court

December 23, 1976 (Abridgement)

(The prosecution in the Kim Chi Ha case unilaterally requested a guilty verdict and ten-year sentence on December 14, 1976. Then, on December 23, by bringing to a close the defense attorney's final arguments and Kim Chi Ha's final three-hour-and-fifteen-minute statement, the court handed down a seven-year sentence for violation of the Anti-Communist Law.

Of the poet's final statement, two hours and thirty minutes deal specifically with the charges against him. The last forty minutes, although not directly related to the case, contain Kim Chi Ha's vision of the unification of South and North Korea. An abridgement of this statement is included below. It has been taken from the notes and memories of persons who attended his trial as spectators.)

As I have said repeatedly, my thought is neither so mature nor organized that it can be given a name. However, if I had to call it something, I would like to call it a philosophy of unification. To reveal contradiction itself, and then to genuinely overcome it, creating a world of friendship and unity—this is my philosophy. For a long time I have dreamed of a unification of God and revolution; of a unification of bread and freedom, earth and heaven, prayer and action. And now I am experiencing this vision more vividly than ever.

This philosophy grows primarily out of my personal experience in having come from among the masses, my life as a poet, and my religious faith. However, it is a fact, and one which increases my confidence, that the same groping path can be discerned in the works of many Korean intellectuals, writers, and scholars of my generation. I believe that this phenomenon is no accident; the very philosophy of unity which I pursue is the claim of our generation, the demand of our people.

The immediate historical problem of the Korean people is the unification of north and south. However, this is not simply a question of linking the territories back together. The authentic unification of the people themselves is the essential basis of the philosophy of unity of which I dream. It is only through unity that our people can live; it is only through unity that we can conquer oppression from within and from without the country, and arrive at a world of true fraternity. This unity can by no means be achieved by makeshift artifice or stratagems, nor by forcing things. What is called for is an entirely new philosophy, an entirely new spirit, and the emergence of a fundamentally new human being. It is for this that I am crying out like a madman in this courtroom.

The ultimate objective of this philosophy of unity is the state of what Christianity calls *koinonia*. But the immediate problem with which we must actually struggle is how, from our present situation, we can bring about a National Democratic Revolution. I have explained the character of this National Democratic Revolution in detail earlier. I have made clear that it is the present regime—this rotten dictatorial power, these exploitative capitalists, this pawn of neocolonial foreign powers—which is the target of this revolution. To bring about the collapse of the Park regime is an extremely difficult task. This regime has a tight hold on all of the nation's power and organizational strength. And in collusion with the immense financial might of the rotten comprador business interests, it receives unlimited support from the neocolonialists. It not only maintains an absurd potential for violence, but it also puts each new bit of information, intelligence, and technology to use for the deception and manipulation of the people of this country.

Those who go to America and Europe and come back with doctorships and professorships head straight for the Blue House [presidential mansion] as soon as they get off the plane. And once they get in, they concentrate on binding the people in wrappings of deceitful cunning. In the midst of all this, what can poor loafers like me accomplish? In fact, in the face of this regime's immense repressive capacities there are hardly any individuals or groups with the strength to carry out the democratic revolution we hope for. In one sense, it may be because of the "mercy" of the regime that I have been able to hold out this far.

Even if the regime carries its oppression to the extreme, however, it will not succeed, for the harder it whips us, the more people there will be to increase our power of resistance. These will be, in a word, the masses of the lower depths —those who have been deprived of even their exhausting life in the village, and who, when they crowd into the city, are unable to enter the exhausted ranks of the industrial laborers and are forced to move to the outskirts with the masses of the unemployed and sell their bodies as day-laborers, thieves, prostitutes, and beggars. Now I have to defend myself against the prosecution's preposterous claim that I advocate a communist proletarian class revolution. In order to show that my thought has some degree of sociological relevance, I have used the term *lumpenproletariat*. But those who I refer to as the masses of the lower depths are the same people the Bible calls "the least of these, my brethren," and Frantz Fanon calls "the wretched of the earth."

Their accumulated resentment cannot be dissipated by any stratagems of the government. The more the government uses its power to oppress them, the greater will be their resentment and the sooner the explosion of their outrage. I know this will be an explosion of tremendous power. As an intellectual and a Christian, how can I ignore this? When the resentment of the people turns into blind violence, the result is a horror. Here the Christian philosophy of nonviolence, and its teaching of love, must be mobilized to awaken the people's consciousness. This must not be carried out in the realm of tactical negotiation and compromise, but must be a true unification. The resentment of the lower depths and the blood of Christ must be joined into one. For those who have suffered under the immorality of starvation and tyranny, this is the way to the restoration of humanity. And I believe that this is the true form of the revolutionary religion, which seeks to put the teachings of Jesus Christ into practice in the modern world.

The division between the north and the south, which has already lasted for an entire generation, is not only the greatest symbol, but also the principal cause that maintains and preserves all the splits and contradictions that control our lives. The established orders of the north and south are equally responsible for preventing the true fraternity common to all humanity from being realized among the people and within the nation. I have no direct experience of the north, but I think that its idolatry and rigidity of thought must naturally be overcome. The dictatorial regimes of the north and south are strengthened by the partition of the country, and they use that strength to maintain their oppressive orders.

The Park government has made a superficial pretense of desiring unification and of promoting dialogue between the north and south, but it has long been known that this was only deception to prolong the regime.

More recently, the government has been publicly maneuvering to stabilize and perpetuate the partition. This Park regime is the greatest direct obstacle to Korean unification and is the faithful servant of the neocolonial powers that desire the continued partition and division of the Korean people. To achieve unification, we must begin by exposing this fact, bringing it out into the open and making it clear. It is entirely natural that the Park regime responds to these efforts of ours with imprisonment and execution. Therefore I think that ultimately, as long as this regime lasts, the only path to unification is the path to West Gate prison. At least I believe that there is no other way for me; my life in prison for the last three years has had its own significance.

However, the disintegration of dictatorship in both the north and the south is inevitable. Given that, and considering all the conditions, I believe that the National Democratic Revolution will occur first in the south. I am no prophet, but I can say with confidence that the day will come soon when the dictatorial regime, which represses and exploits the people, will disintegrate to nothing; that freedom of speech, press, and assembly will be resurrected; that the Anti-Communist Law will be abolished; and that all the young people, the young flowers who have been held captive in prison, will be released. The bright Spring of Athens is coming to call on the Republic of Korea. And when the Spring of Athens has visited the south, it will then urge change upon the north. Whether in the form of intra-party democracy, or whether through some other form of popular awakening, in any case, the Spring of Prague will come to the north as well. In this way the Spring of Athens and the Spring of Prague will gradually envelop the entire Korean peninsula, and a single, great overflowing Spring will be achieved in our land. The approach—and the welcoming—of this bright, radiant Spring: This is the unification of which I dream.

Of course, to achieve this unification, the efforts of many politicians, revolutionaries, intellectuals, and scholars will be required. But more than anything, I believe it is the unsophisticated and uncorrupted youth who will actually be at the center of this meeting of two Springs. At the DMZ, the guns will cease to fire, and like monkeys, rabbits, pheasants, and deer romping at play, the youth of the north and the south will come together, talk, sing, and dance until dawn, groping for a new philosophy and stepping into a whole new world of friendship. In the expansion of this realm of friendship the efforts of the older, responsible generation will come to fruition, and soon it will sweep over the whole peninsula. The new philosophy and the new human being born here will not stop at the unification of the Korean peninsula, but will become the guides to the self-restoration of all peoples, and to the perfection of humanity, through the self-awakening of the peoples of the Third World. And they will contribute, in the words of the prophet Isaiah, to the hammering of swords into plowshares and the realization of peace in the world.

Some might think that these are simply the ravings of a madman. However, in my vision of unification, I am convinced that the signs of the approaching radiant Spring on this peninsula can already be seen. In my confinement, deprived of all freedom in my narrow cell, this vision of unification brings me happiness. Although this is a happiness in the midst of suffering, it is more precious even than the happiness which can be bestowed by a woman. For the sake of this vision of unification I am prepared to struggle to the last and to undergo whatever ordeals may come.

I have already gone into detail to refute the groundless and unjust charges that the prosecution has brought against me. Needless to say, I am innocent. Even so, I don't care whether or not I am released. During this time, in my heart, I have experienced much unrest. I have considered many possibilities, such as whether I would be released or granted parole. But now I have discarded all such thoughts. My heart is happy and at peace. My only desire is that the decision will be made for the sake of truth and not just for me.

In conclusion, I would like to say one more thing: I feel truly sorry about those in the People's Revolutionary Party case. Although it is too late for the ones who have already died, those who are alive must be released immediately! Those like myself, who acted originally out of conviction and then were punished, were prepared for and can comprehend what has happened. And though I am a little embarrassed to say so, we are even respected by our guards and fellow-prisoners. But what must be the bitterness of those who, under absurd, framed-up charges, were executed or are still suffering in prison to this day? Not one of us who complacently abandons the effort to save them can escape the accusation of being an accomplice to this regime.

Finally, I would like to take the opportunity to express my profound appreciation to the following people who, despite being in prison themselves, went on a hunger strike on my behalf. Fr. Hahm Sei Woong, Fr. Moon Jung Hyun, Fr. Shin Hyun Bong, Rev. Yun Bang Ung, Prof. Lee Moon Young, Prof. Suh Nam Dong, Prof. Moon Dong Wham, Mr. Kim Dae Jung, and others whose names I don't even know. And there are many students, younger than myself, who are suffering because of me for circulating my Declaration of Conscience. I want them set free at once. It breaks my heart that they are still in prison.

Tomorrow will be the day our Lord comes. It is a meaningful day of promise, for me personally as well. I pray that God's grace be with everyone; as for those most responsible for this regime, beginning with Mr. Park Chung Hee, and including all high government officials, I pray that God's blessing will pour down upon them like a great, silent snow, and cover them with its drifts.

—Translated by the Japanese Council for Justice and Peace

Torture Road—1974

I

I was arrested on Huksan Island last year [1974], at dawn, on April 25. I was staying at a tourist hotel, a place I had stayed before, as assistant director for the movie *The Blue Girl.*

Police Sgt. Min, of the Huksan Island branch of the Mokp'o police station, after greeting me cordially, handcuffed my wrists and transferred me to a ferry. I sat on the deck staring at the dark gloomy sea stretching endlessly before me, as if I had lost my soul.

When the boat docked in Mokp'o harbor, I thought for a moment I heard the sobbing sounds of a flute playing in a low key. Native home, ten years, I have yearned for you. Native home, I return to you in handcuffs. Oh, what you have been to me, Mount Yudal. How I have yearned for you. How shabby I am as I stand before you, Mount Yudal. Suddenly, sobbing began to burst out from the deepest recesses of my heart. Blood-soaked yellow hills, veined with grief at every turn.[1] You, the mother of my poem. The rake-like emaciated hands of my grandmother eating *sajapab.*[2] The wailing of my grandfather, pounding his head against the grass, while burying my nephew Chinguk, who died from starvation. The blood lump-like eyes of Tt'ukeng, who came down from Mount Binyo[3] in fury, brandishing a bamboo spear. The unforgettable look of Ch'angnam gulping down his tears, while going over the corpses one by one in the dark, dark night, searching for his father who had been buried alive. Oh, I have returned to the native home of those memories in handcuffs.

Barely suppressing tears, I crossed the gangplank and saw the sunburned faces of the fishmonger women, weary of life, standing in groups at the pier. They were looking at my handcuffs, as if I were a thief or an armed robber. Yet on those faces I found sympathy for me—as a misfortunate one, who bore the cruel fate and like themselves starved and shivered. Among these faces, I discovered my warm and hearty friends of my native home, who greeted my return. Yes, I have now returned to my native home.

I have come back to the warmth and to my own blood. Holding my grudges and crazing anger to me, the lament of my gut—like a handcuffed son from the cursed land of Cholla Province and like the poet of the disdainfully treated locality. I greet you native home, to whom I have returned by the same dusty road of ten years ago. In greeting, I began to feel a smile slowly returning inside my heart.

II

The strange colored rooms of Section 6 at the Central Intelligence Agency. The feeling of the dismal, coldly lit rooms that always give me the strange feeling I felt when waking up from a nightmare and looking at the glaring white wall. Those dreadful rooms that deny every tender memory and hope. Those strange colored rooms that chill and give you the illusion of some shrivelled body from remote antiquity. A body that died with an open mouth from brutal torture, hanging on the wall just as it was, decaying for several hundred years. Those square, plain rooms that cannot see day from night that are always dimly lit. The same-size, barren, square rooms. We were locked in these rooms for ten days, fifteen days, a month. I don't know for how long. From moment to moment, without end, we writhed, confronting life or death.

"Mysterious torture road of candle light, paradox of overcoming death by choosing death."

There is no going home
after having stepped inside
and slept here
a sleep that goes deep
into the flesh

The room of sleep
that dizziness of looking into an abyss
even if you were able to stand
upon your feet,
there is no going home

Even if you rise
see the blood on the wall,
like an ancient scream
chilling, chilling

Pushing hard,
even if you rise
there is still no going home

Oh, rough road, a vagabond would
never come here twice

The sound of footsteps,
of those hard heels, heavy on the ceiling
all night long
back and forth above me
invisible faces,
hands, and gestures

That room that shouts
and roars with laughter
that white room—
that dizziness of an abyss

Eyes widened in fright
by the agony of torn out nails
flesh ripped apart
aching and screaming to go on living
because screaming is the desire to live
the emaciated soul revives
stands along the road, walks away

Untimely, untimely,
the friends who fell dead
into sleep covered with shame
they fell into sleep
untimely, untimely

Under whippings, kickings, sneerings,
the friends who fell dead
the friends who had once smiled at me
who had once cried and embraced me
such good friends

You will never go home
if you doze once in that room
you shall never return
bruised black and blue
bruised black and blue
unless you writhe and resist
like a madman,
you will never go home

Windy rough road
my brothers and vagabonds
this is not a place
to come to twice

In these rooms, death clung to us every moment, every moment. In these rooms, we confronted death, struggled against death, finding inner freedom by overcoming death, or the humiliation of a useless fall by surrendering. Nineteen hundred and seventy-four was a time of death for everyone connected with this affair, and it was a head-on struggle with death.

Mysterious torture road of candle light, paradox of overcoming death by choosing death. This was our task: to comprehend this mysterious torture road. In the death room, where the question of death clung to us, I learned of the birth of my son. Oh, God, for the first time I understood your will.

III

Out of the darkness
someone calls me
the cell across from the rusty iron bars
black, red darkness
a pair of glaring eyes crouching
in the darkness
Oh, that silence calls me
gasps of breath rattling with phlegm
calls me

On the rainy day
of the low grey sky
how many times was
that sound cut off
by the cooing of the pigeons
on the roof

How many times
how many times
was that sound cut off
by the sound of prison locks
by the sound of the bugle

by the sound of the footsteps
endlessly calling me

Blood-stained underwear
hung on the iron bars
endless nights of cellars
writhing, white souls
the cries of shredded bodies

Shaking my head
Oh, shaking my head
that calm silence is
calling me
calling my blood
to refuse, to refuse
all lies

Out of the darkness,
on the rainy day
of the low grey sky
out of the darkness
of that bruised black red
black red flesh
my wide staring eyes

On the rainy day of the low grey sky, the phlegm rattling voice was calling my name. I went to the excrement barrel in the corner and scrunched up against the window. I asked, who is calling me.

"I am Ha Chae Wan."

"Who is Ha Chae Wan?"

"Of the People's Revolutionary Party."[4]

In this way our secret conversations began, over the windows between my cell no. 15 on the second floor and his cell no. 17 on the first floor.

"Was there really a PRP?"

"Of course not; the government dreamed it all up."

"Then on what basis are they holding you in prison?"

"For torture."

"Was the torture bad?"

"They ruptured my intestines. It was a mess."

"What the hell, what the hell," I clacked my tongue.

"The KCIA said, 'We know this is rough on you, but it is a political problem so just try to stand it a little longer.' "

"Is that so."

Later, in July, while I was crouching down in line and waiting for my turn for a medical check-up, I saw a man squatting on the other side of the line. He was a short, slightly curly haired man with knife scars on his face. He was squatting on his haunches. He could have been a tough guy with his fists in the old days.

"Are you Kim Chi Ha?" he asked, patting my shoulder.

"I am, but who are you?"

"I am Ha Chae Wan," he said, pointing with his right thumb to his breast.

In this way, Ha Chae Wan, with whom I had a brief exchange, related the same story of torture, in a low, quick voice, while intently studying the guards' faces. I felt as if he were hugging me tightly like a hundred-year-old bosom friend, meeting me in hell. His phlegm gasping breath sound was a ghastly echo in my ear, like the cry of some vengeful demon. He and I carefully studied the guards' faces.

On another day at about that time, when I was making a court appearance, an inmate asked me, "Are you Kim Chi Ha?"

When I answered "Yes, I am but . . . ", he introduced himself, "I am Lee Su Byong."

"Are you Lee Su Byong who wrote 'On Savagery'? "

"Yes."

"What has happened to you?"

"I am ashamed of myself for I have been dragged into here without doing anything good for the people. I am sorry . . . for doing forced labor here defaming the great student movement."

"I see."

In the court room I heard Lee Kang Ch'ol, a student of Kyongbuk University, saying clearly in a distinct voice, "I have never known or even heard of the term PRP. By my refusal to acknowledge 'my good knowledge' of it, I was repeatedly subjected to electric torture in the presence of the prosecutor." This story confirmed for me that the label PRP was a fabrication, a lie made up out of their barbaric inhumanity and their need to torture.

Later, one day I sat against the cell wall, suffering from endless torment, my whole body trembling from anger.

My blood calls out
refuse
refuse all lies.

To refuse? Yes, outright rejection. To expose the truth buried in the darkness to the daylight? To refuse lies? That is right. The riddle of the light in Hölderlin's poem. That riddle was the refusal. Yes, that is what it was.

IV

The death sentence was proclaimed. Both Kim Byong Kon and I laughed. Byong Kon began his last statement. "This is an honor," he uttered as soon as he opened his mouth. What in the world does that mean, "an honor." What is this all about? To utter words "this is an honor" by a person receiving the death penalty. What the hell are you talking about, Kim Byong Kon? I felt I was sucked into a state of enigmatic shock. Did I really understand what these words meant?

The death penalty clearly means they will kill you. They are going to stop your life and you will be extinguished. You are going to breathe your last breath and everything will come to an end. Flowers, wind, gentle-eyed sweethearts, the beautiful greenish smoke of supper cooking from chimneys of the foothill villages, against the full sunset. The compassionate face of your wrinkled, aged mother, the warmth of your father's gnarled, earth-beaten hands. All, everything, instantly, without any trace is going to disappear. Why then do you say, "This is an honor?"

Are these the words of saints? Are we saints? Are these sarcastic words uttered with the assumption they will not dare to execute us? Can we, who know their barbarism too well, flirt with the luxury of sarcasm? No. It is not that. What do these words then mean? We at last conquered our terror of death. That is right. That is truly right. Writhing every moment and everyday in blood all over that hell, we have overcome.

It was not Kyong Sok, individually, Byong Kon, individually, or I, individually, who overcame. But all of us triumphed collectively. And triumphing, we elected the seal of eternally divine grace on our death. By accepting death, we overcame death. By choosing death, we collectively gained eternity.

With deep feeling, we gazed into the brilliant flame of truthful life, which began to burn inside our collectively chained flesh. It was our historical moment. No, it was not just something of this world. It was religious inspiration. But it was not only that. It was the height of artistic vision. No, it cannot be expressed in words. It was a glittering zenith of wholeness of all human values and sublimities. I began to feel as if I were in touch with the mystery of the spirit.

At that time, for some reason, the word—"the power of political imagination"—suddenly flashed back into my mind. I felt these words were deeply carved into the bottom of my heart like red-blue hot brands. Yes, "the power of political imagination": the wedding of politics and art in the highest sense of the words. It is not an absurd relationship.

Unity. Yes. At last, I have bridged the gap in a single leap between my mass movements, political activities, and artistic creation—the gap that had driven me insane for so long. The definitive answer to this enigma has been presented to me through the torture road. An extravagant, extravagant moment. At that time, I muttered to myself, "I thank you," and those almost unspeakable words, "I am honored."

V

This waiting a long, long time, forgetting what one waits for. Just waiting, endless waiting. No other way but waiting. This waiting that drives you crazy. Waiting in hope that someone at the cost of his life, at the cost of his life, even only once . . . to smash down this waiting, vexing, blood-burning, this long, long time. Even that one small blade of grass on the prison roof does not move. That time of no wind, no sound, no color—life imprisonment. Excremental water-filled barrel, the guard's endless cursings, bone-breaking labor. Gritty boiled barley, rotten salted fish guts. Squeaky, desperate, running sound of an outdated cutting machine made in Japan in 1945. Thieves, armed robbers, brutal rapists and murderers beating each other up. One cut his belly open on the roof, others screamed, while holding their fingers caught in the gears. And the mind falls and falls into a bottomless hole beyond all hope, from which it never returns. Thus, nothing but futile, bloody waiting: hell.

Welcome, splendid Chi Ha, Chi Ha. Welcome to this hell. This prison is another name for your name. This hell is

"Even that one small blade of grass on the prison roof does not move. The time of no wind, no sound, no color—life imprisonment."

another name for your native earth. This is the place you had to come to. You, everything of yours, every fingernail, every strand of hair. Give them all up. The cursed body flesh. The purged soul. The day when the liberating white flag raises with the so-called thieves, armed robbers, brutal rapists, and murderers. That day of glittering ascension to heaven. That day of storms and angry waves, the end of the world. This awful waiting at the end of the world—prison. I am for the first time, for the first time, barely, because of my rancor in the deep recesses of my mind, completely united, both inside and out. That is right.

We are united by those flashing handcuffs which chained all of us. We are fused together in the boiling blast furnace in the dark, dark, darkness—the Yongdongp'o prison. It was a presentiment of yellow light that united us . . . by smashing down all discriminations: ideologies, colors, dialects, standard languages, the rich and the poor.

Dreaming
dreaming a bird
become a bird and wherever
dream madly, dream of flying

On a grease-messy straw mat on the workshop floor
become rusty tools, become rubbish
clenching a severed finger

Dream a bird
even battered closing eyes dream madly
become a white kite
become blossoming green barley fields
madly become a bird, become a grosbeak
red reminders, countlessly
become birds and do not return after you disappear

Endlessly
unknowable
outside of the workshop gate
wherever
endlessly

Amount in arrears, adjustment results,
reports, individual annual income, collection records,
receipts, minutes, total tabulation, tax notices
leaving my hands

Become blue birds
or crows
disappear, go away
do not return and leave nothing behind

Dumped on a grease-messy straw mat on the workshop floor
at twenty, the springtime of youth
made in Japan in 1945
Oh, oh, I am a worn-out Kawamoto cutter

Print out, print out, cut, snapped
panting, weary, emaciated, staggering
becomes rusty tools, battered and insane
even so
dreams a bird

When clenching a cut-off finger
becomes pretty multi-colored patches
becomes a pinwheel
becomes a red tag dump glued
onto the wall of my native home
becomes the flower bier bearing the coffin
by all means, by all means
becomes a whistle wailing night train

Dreams
dreams a bird
becomes a bird and wherever
dreams madly, dreams of flying
become the singer Namchin, become the singer Namchin

On that stage
to these crowds
I want to shout
by becoming that glittering, glittering trumpet,
illuminated by stage spotlights
Hey, world—bursting, crying until
the throat tears apart
torn to pieces, torn to pieces, and then nothing—
disappears

Become the singer Namchin on a stage where
there is no stinking poor peoples' rice
not even overtime work
become a bird

Hey, fingers, I'd like to go away and disappear
nothing, nothing, leaving behind nothing
not even a single memory

This cut-off twenty years of mine
becomes a cinema
neither day nor night

The dark Yongdongp'o
abandoned dumbstruck machine
made in Japan in 1945
Oh, I am a worn-out Kawamoto cutter

Today, I am a small bloody finger that leaves the prison gate. I had waited a long time for the day both body and soul would be set free together. But I have been tricked by a cunning devil. I am a cut-off finger thrown out of the prison gate because of that trick. My severed finger is an empty hollow. It is nothing but an empty shell of flesh that spirit has left. My soul—that had been at the point of such union—where is it now? Only a wind blowing in the dark street of night. Why is your body alone blowing with the wind, travelling in the dead of night? Where did you leave your soul? Oh, my friends who are not yet liberated. Those friends whose ruptured intestines were spilled out by torture, . . . and those who are crouching in the darkness, with their eyes glaring and gasping with phlegm-rattling breath. My affectionate friends in the prison—"thieves and robbers." Those soldiers who left the peninsula, wept at the moment of separation and later massacred innocent villagers in Vietnam. I was no other than they. They were no other than I. Right. That is right. I left my soul behind in prison. An empty shell left the prison. My soul is there, crying. Sobbing madly, it is calling out to my flesh . . . to liberate, to be together, to be united. It is crying to meet again. My soul is waving a hand to me to come home. And my empty flesh, alone, all alone is blowing and walking here and there on the grey blustering street.

Let's go, to search for my soul. Let's go, go and open the prison gates and set my soul free. Embrace in liberation until the tears run down on my face. To unite, to be one, to be together.

My flesh will fight until it meets with my soul. Smashed with beatings into fine, fine pieces blown away on the wind—until then, my flesh will fight.

—Translated by Chong Sun Kim and Shelly Killen

NOTES

1. Cholla Province, where Kim Chi Ha was born, is covered with red-smeared yellow soil, which symbolizes his sentiments toward Korea. The yellow soil represents the bloody, tragic history of Korea, where massacres were common and human corpses landscaped the country. The yellow soil was placed inside a coffin with the deceased so their spirits would revive and travel to the next world.

2. *Sajapab*. When a person died in Korea, white cloths were thrown on the roof of the home, and food was placed outside the gate so the deceased would have nourishment during the long journey to the next world. It was the custom not to eat this food. The fact that Kim Chi Ha's grandmother partook of this food indicates the extremity of the poverty.

3. There were many massacres at Mount Binyo during the Korean War. It was occupied by the anti-Communists in the daytime and by Communists at night. People from the surrounding villages were subjected to murder, torture, and rape. Prior to the Korean War, it was associated with fierce guerrilla struggles.

4. After the fall of South Vietnam, Park Chung Hee's repression of civil liberties in South Korea increased. April 19 is the anniversary of the student revolution that toppled the Syngman Rhee regime in 1960; afraid of another major student outbreak, Park issued "Emergency Measure No. Seven" on April 8, 1974, and ordered the shutdown of the universities, which were in the midst of demonstrations. Meanwhile, the government began to arrest students and others from different walks of life. Among them, eight received the death penalty on the grounds that they were connected with the "People's Revolutionary Party"; others received long-term sentences. After a year in jail, the eight were executed, despite the fact that the death sentence could be appealed according to law.

The "People's Revolutionary Party" is a fabrication, and the execution was designed to set an example for those who in any way opposed the regime. When the judge proclaimed the death penalty there were neither defendants nor defense lawyers in the court. Word had spread that the men were unable to stand in court because of the horrible torture they had undergone, or because they were executed before a court hearing. The families of the victims demanded a final meeting before the execution. The authorities promised them a meeting, which was to be held on April 9, 1975. The families waited in front of the prison on that day from 9 A.M. However, the radio announced that they were already executed.

Having no recourse in the face of these barbaric acts, the families asked the authorities to surrender the victims' bodies. The authorities promised to deliver the bodies the next day. But the following morning they announced a twelve-hour postponement. After this time they promised to take charge themselves of cremation or burial. The church had prepared farewell prayers for the victims and the relatives were preparing funeral rites, but there were no bodies. During the commotion between the authorities and the families of the victims over the bodies, someone notified the families that a bier had passed through the West Gate and was heading toward the cremation site. They ran and stopped the car that was carrying the body on a street in Unp'yong-dong. Friends, including Catholic priests, lay down in front of the wheels of the car and demanded the body. They argued and protested for four hours and finally they received the body, but police came later and snatched it away. Although five other bodies were not allowed to be seen, some people who had by chance briefly seen them at the cremation site testified to viewing the marks of chains and whips as well as severed fingers and flesh torn apart.

The Gold-Crowned Jesus

Time: Winter, 1971

Place: Ghetto in a small Korean City

Cast:
Jesus Christ
Priest, *about sixty years old*
Nun, *about twenty-five*
Leper, *middle-aged*
Beggar, *middle-aged*
Prostitute, *about thirty*
Company president, *about forty-five and corpulent*
Policeman, *about thirty*
University student, *about twenty-three*

ACT I

Curtain rises. A Christ-pietà figure can be seen in silhouette against light filtering through a window off stage. Center stage is a small table with a large jacketed Bible on it. A PRIEST *and* NUN *are on the right and left side of the table respectively. They sit without moving and stare at each other in silence. A song accompanied by guitar music can be heard in the background:*

That frozen sky
That frozen field
Even the sun has lost its light
Oh, that poor, dark, dark street

Where did you come from
People with emaciated faces . . . ?
Why are you running around?
Running around in search of what?
Those eyes
Those emaciated hands

There is no native earth
There is no place to rest your tired bodies
There is no place even for a grave
In the heart of winter
I have been abandoned
I have been abandoned

Ah, the street
The lonely street
The hands that refuse
Those frozen dark, dark streets of betrayals

Where can it be?
Where is the heavenly kingdom?
Over on the other side of death?
Green forest of the four seasons
Can it be there?

I will go there after death
I will go there after death
I will abandon this suffering life
I will go there after death

Endless winter
Darkness of the abyss that I cannot bear

This tragic time and tide
This endless, endless poverty
This empty, cold world
I cannot bear it any longer

Where can he be?
Where can he be?
Where is Jesus?
That frozen sky
That frozen field
Even the sun has lost its light
That dark, dark, poor street
Where can he be?
Where can he be?
He who could save us
Where can he be?

Oh, Jesus
Now here with us
Oh, Jesus, with us

Oh, Jesus
Now here with us
Oh, Jesus, with us

Oh, Jesus
Now here with us
Oh, Jesus, with us

(When the sound of the song stops, the PRIEST *utters a loud sigh. The* NUN *begins to speak, eyeing him sharply.)*

NUN: Should I tell her to come back? *(pause)* Should I?

PRIEST: What did you say?

NUN: Magdalene Hong, she wants to do penance.

PRIEST: I see *(pause)*. What does she do?

NUN: She is one of the poor people, a prostitute.

PRIEST: Prostitute *(sighs)*. Tell her to come next time. And her donation?

NUN: Not much.

PRIEST: Why is that?

NUN: Because she is poor. She is one of the *poor* people, you know.

PRIEST: Poor? *(sighs wearily)* That's possible.

NUN: And some members of the Peace Committee for the Achievement of Social Justice want to come to see you at nine this evening.

PRIEST: At nine o'clock *(looks at his wristwatch)*. Just what kind of business are they about?

NUN: It's about the social justice problem.

PRIEST: What are you talking about?

NUN *(stubbornly)*: It's about the issue of social justice.

PRIEST: What issue of social justice? Is it about the demonstration?

NUN: It seems so.

PRIEST: It must be about the demonstration. Demonstrations! Demonstrations!

NUN: What will you do? Will you help them?

PRIEST: Well . . . well . . .

NUN: Father, the demonstration *must* be carried out. Their claim is valid. Isn't it?

PRIEST: How is it valid?

NUN: How is it valid? And where are these poor people to go in such a harsh winter? They wouldn't have the vaguest idea about how to feed themselves. How can they suddenly arrange for new houses if their present homes are torn down?

PRIEST: I understand all that. But wouldn't helping them be

the same as encouraging prostitution? Aren't you asking me to approve of it? Aren't you actually condoning prostitution?

NUN: But it's not their fault.

PRIEST: No? Then whose fault is it?

NUN: Are they liars because they want to be liars? They have become what they are because they were poor and society is unjust.

PRIEST: Some things must be as they are. Even the state cannot help *these* poor.

NUN: Then who will help them? No efforts have been or will be made to help them. The state has rejected them, as has the church. What is to become of them?

PRIEST: The church has always taken care of them.

NUN: A pittance only. You're talking about rescue work. Do you really think that helped them?

PRIEST: Are you saying that it didn't help them?

NUN: No, but the real issue lies elsewhere.

PRIEST: What are you talking about? *(sighs)*

NUN: They need help with more essential problems. Their rights and dignity as human beings. Our task should be to help them not only recognize these rights but to acquire them. Giving them goods is equivalent to treating a symptom and ignoring the cause of an illness. To nurture the psychological habit of dependency is only to weaken them. We have to think in terms of solutions to these problems, otherwise . . .

PRIEST *(sighs)*: My head gets dizzy when I talk with her. A prostitutes' ghetto is bad. It causes moral disorder. And demonstrations against society are bad because they cause confusion.

NUN: You can't say that.

PRIEST: You're saying that prostitution is not bad?

NUN: I mean the demonstration. And about the prostitutes' ghetto. They are like that in order to suvive! Like the rest of the poor, schooling was not open to them. Even the Bible says . . .

PRIEST *(cutting in quickly, triumphantly):* That's a different issue. This is about a demonstration.

NUN: But that's why they are demonstrating.

PRIEST: If that's why, then again, to help them is to condone prostitution.

NUN: I've already agreed it is not right. But if the ghetto is torn down, then an alternative should be provided for them.

PRIEST: By whom?

NUN: By the government.

PRIEST *(triumphantly):* That is a political matter. The church is not supposed to get involved in such things.

NUN: Why not?

PRIEST: The church cannot disregard the national laws.

NUN: Even if the national laws go against the laws of God?

PRIEST: The authorities are not unreasonable and they must be tearing them down for a very good reason. We have to trust them *(pause).* What else can we do?

NUN: We cannot trust them. They have never concerned themselves with alternatives or solutions. They've misled us several times before.

PRIEST: The place is a breeding ground for prostitution.

NUN *(impassioned):* Den of prostitution, den of prostitution, den of prostitution, that's all you say, but human beings live there. They are not beasts. Mary Magdalene was a prostitute and look how Christ treated her. And as far as the church and the prostitutes are concerned any number of church members live off their hard-earned money. How can we then turn away from them?

PRIEST: I can't help doing what I do. Just what do you want me to do? Are you asking me to lead a demonstration? How can a priest lead a demonstration? Anyway, I'm against demonstrations. They cause trouble.

NUN *(a scornful smile on her face):* What *would* you do? Have you ever taken a positive position, committed yourself to action of any kind?

PRIEST: So! You are trying to ridicule me, saying I am without courage. A nun like a doubting believer is trying to . . . *(avoids her while trying to calm down).* All we can do is pray. Through prayer all the troubles of the world can be eliminated *(gaining momentum).* Through prayer people will receive eternity. That's all we can know. Prostitution, prostitution dens, and then a *demonstration.* And because of this we then have lepers, beggars, thieves, and other undesirables hanging around. It is all a filthy mess.

NUN: Even lepers, beggars, thieves, undesirables, prostitutes, and day-to-day workers are the children of the Lord. Jesus particularly loved these people.

PRIEST: *You* are trying to teach *me* something? Absolutely no, no, to a demonstration.

NUN: Then you reject the encyclicals *Mater et Magistra*, *Pacem in Terris*, decisions made at ecumenical conferences, statements made by bishops about the achievement of social justice, the various decrees of the Holy Father, as just useless talk?

PRIEST: I don't have any time *(looking at his wristwatch and standing up).*

NUN: Are you going to see them or not? *(standing up, following the priest).*

PRIEST: See who?

NUN: The members of the Committee for Social Justice.

PRIEST: I don't have any time. I have a previous engagement *(obviously making it up as he goes).* An important business appointment. Very important business. It's absolutely necessary that I go to my appointment. Now!

NUN: I see. I'll tell them that.

PRIEST: No, don't tell them that. It's like this . . . let me see . . . and . . .

NUN: I understand. Well then . . . (*turns to leave*)

PRIEST (*relieved*): Thank you. Send in Teresa. That white fur muffler I received as a gift? I must wear it around my neck. Where is it? Send Teresa in, quickly, I don't have much time.

NUN: Teresa has left.

PRIEST: Left? Where did she go?

NUN: To her home.

PRIEST: Why?

NUN: She said her salary was too little and the work was too hard. She left a little while ago, after supper.

PRIEST: For good?

NUN: Yes, for good!

PRIEST: Well, well, then (*changing the subject*). Where is the white sheep muffler I received as a gift?

NUN: I don't know. Why don't you find it yourself? (*leaves from stage*).

PRIEST: How can I go out? I must wear it. I must wear it around my neck. How can I go out without it? (*After remaining standing, he sits on a chair and speaks in a strange, low voice.*) What is to become of me? What will . . . I wasn't like this before . . . I wasn't like this when I was young.

CURTAIN

ACT II

Street Scene. Darkness. Song from Act I is repeated. The stage slowly lightens as song ends. The Christ-pietà statue is still visible. A LEPER *and a* BEGGAR *are sitting back-to-back in the middle of the stage.*

BEGGAR: It's cold, I'm shivering.
LEPER: Where?
BEGGAR: My jaws.
LEPER: And it's still early in the evening.
BEGGAR: How about you?
LEPER: I'm trembling too.
BEGGAR: Where?
LEPER: In all my muscles and joints.
BEGGAR *(rubbing his arms, legs, to warm them):* Is there any way *not* to be cold?
LEPER: You wouldn't be cold if you were rich.
BEGGAR: Let's pretend we are rich then.
LEPER: Sure. You go first. What would you like?
BEGGAR *(ponders):* A room that is warm all over. With warm floors.
LEPER: Ah! A room that's heated from below.
BEGGAR: And a crackling charcoal fire.
LEPER *(picking up on the idea):* With delicious barbecue spare ribs turning on a spit.
BEGGAR: Something to drink. A cup of soju wine.
LEPER: Then, if the spare ribs are lean, some cow intestines as well.
BEGGAR: Then, if my belly's not filled, chicken entrails.
LEPER *(feeding the dream):* Heart, liver, kidney, chitlings, and tripe.

(Here the BEGGAR *and* LEPER *turn around and begin to mime the actions of cooking on a barbecue grill.)*

BEGGAR: We'll eat them sizzling from the grill.

LEPER: We'll put red hot sauce on the pork.

BEGGAR: And lay it on the grill to barbecue.

LEPER AND BEGGAR *(in unison and interacting as they improvise turning the meat, finger licking, etc.):*

Sizzling, sizzling, sizzling, sizzling,
sizzling, sizz . . . si . . . sizzling.
Such mouth-watering flavor
burned out by a cup of soju
warms the guts, the limbs relax.
Just the thought of it and my god-damned mouth waters.
My eyeballs spin, it makes the hunchback dance,
and the world shrinks to the size of a coin.

(LEPER *and* BEGGAR *move bodies to rhythm of following words as if singing a song.)*

Ninano, nilliya, nino,
What a delight.
What a pleasure—Chihwacha—chott'a
Chihwacha—chott'a

BEGGAR *(dropping game, back to reality):* Aw, what the hell! My ass and a dog's nose! I'm shivering all over.

LEPER: It's daybreak. I'm shivering all over.

(The following takes on a mock ritualistic quality.)

BEGGAR: Let's make a fire. A *divine* cigarette butt, if you please. *(He extends his palm to the leper.)*

LEPER: Sure, *divinely* with me.

BEGGAR: Get it out *divinely*.

LEPER: It's coming out most *sacredly (passes the butt).*

BEGGAR *(holding it up)*: It's a ship's mast.

LEPER: It's a twin mast.

BEGGAR *(taking a tinder box out of his pocket):* Here comes a strip of paper from a good Korean floor.*

*Reference to heavily oiled paper used on earthen floors in Korea.

LEPER: Here comes a head *(gets out a tinder box).*
BEGGAR: Like a bride and bridegroom.
LEPER: And now for the union *(strikes a light).* Chorus!
BEGGAR *(solemnly):* A virgin is ruined.
LEPER: But the guy is okay.
BEGGAR *(looks at the butt):* Just the right shade of red this lipstick.
LEPER: Ah, the scent is really strong now.
BEGGAR: Could it have been a fox's?
LEPER: It was a cicada's.
BEGGAR: I like a fox.
LEPER: I like a cicada.*
BEGGAR: What's good about a cheap whore?
LEPER: She has to be good because she comes from my world.
BEGGAR: I like a rich chick. Light white skin . . . fertile and fleshy, lots of glittering jewels. Perhaps a colorful silk dress. Of course, lying back, very seductive in a big fancy car. Very suggestive. Really fine. Ah, and those big blinking, sexy eyes.
LEPER: Damn you, that's not seductive. It's the taste of a radish sick with a cold. Since ancient times, for a chick to be a real chick she has to have vivid eyes, her cheeks solid and shining like an apple . . . and a nice big ass . . . sulky breasts . . . and when she's angry, she should be like a viper. Ah, but when she gives, she tastes like a pear. You fool, what you described is a fox; this is a cicada.
BEGGAR *(a little sulky):* I don't care. I like a rich chick!
LEPER: Yeah, well go ahead, try *real* hard. Just one look at that screwed-up face, like a pasty-faced foreigner's, and the first rich chick will shape you up, real fast *(snaps his fingers at beggar)* and love you madly *(laughs).* Go ahead, try it, and good luck.

*A "fox" is a sly, attractive, affluent, spoiled, sharp-tongued, unattainable woman; a "cicada" is relatively unattractive, shrill as the cicada, and more accessible than the "fox."

BEGGAR: Day is already dawning. But, hey, don't say that . . . because in my dream, everything can be as I want it to be.

LEPER: Well, I guess you're right.

(BEGGAR *and* LEPER *begin to sing together.)*

Dream a dream, dream a dream
In our dream we can be rich
We'll live in a great lordly mansion
We'll be very well fed and clothed
We'll enjoy a merry life

We'll enjoy a merry life
There'll be lots and lots of women
All beautiful like actresses
We'll make them our mistresses
To us they will belong
By eating ginseng, antlers,
along with some seal testicles
We'll live for a thousand million years

But . . .
This is a cold and cruel world
Why were we born at all?

BEGGAR: A beggar's life is hard and grim.

LEPER: Yes, but I was born a leper.

(They continue to sing, but BEGGAR *begins to act out, satirically, mockingly, but with humor, the things the song describes.)*

Dream a dream, dream a dream
In our dream we're top officials

Shantung suits and silk cravats
Riding around in a fancy car
Sticking out our bellies
In and out of private clubs
And living just like princes
Dream a dream, dream a dream . . .

Gaksori singers,* people like us
Were here again last year
Bringing their ribald songs
Having survived another cruel year
They returned to sing again.
Ehya Ulloriya Ho Coliya Ulloriya
Quickly gone over the Arirang Hill†

(Song ends here with disgusted spitting)

BEGGER and LEPER *(in unison):* Damn! Why are we the ones who must carry the rope the police use to bind the criminals!

LEPER: Damn this world where you must live by begging.

BEGGAR: Damn this world where death comes mostly and quickest to the poor.

LEPER: Damn this world where execution is inflicted even on a corpse.

BEGGAR: Damn! Blast! Damn!

BEGGAR and LEPER: Damn this world in which death strikes from all sides.

BEGGAR: Where thunder and lightning strike you.

LEPER: Die from malaria, plague, or cholera.

BEGGAR: Where you can freeze to death.

*The Gaksori are beggars and lepers who sing vulgar songs in the streets and markets to beg money.

†Legendary hill representing the essence and sentiment of the Korean people.

LEPER: Die from a fall, die from slipping, die from burns.

BEGGAR: Die from disease, die from old age.

LEPER: Die like a dog!

BEGGAR: Damn this subhuman world where you must live by begging *(sound of disgusted spitting)*.

LEPER: I'm shivering.

BEGGAR: I'm shivering.

BEGGAR and LEPER *(in unison):* Shivering all over.

BEGGAR: Why is it cold?

LEPER: Because it's winter.

BEGGAR: Is there any way *not* to be cold?

LEPER: Only if you become rich.

BEGGAR: Shussh . . . be silent. Someone is coming.

LEPER: Is it a bloated stomach? Fat cat?

BEGGAR: No.

LEPER: Is it a leech?

BEGGAR: No.

LEPER: Is it a nightsoil fly?

BEGGAR: No.

LEPER: Is it a tax collector?

BEGGAR: No.

LEPER: Is it a night heron?

BEGGAR: No.

LEPER: Is it slippery moss?

BEGGAR: No.

LEPER: What is it then?

BEGGAR *(giving a clue):* It's wearing a black uniform.

LEPER *(surprised):* What? A crow?

BEGGAR *(another clue):* A crow without a nightstick.

LEPER: Skirt or pants?

BEGGAR: Skirt.

LEPER: I see. Well day has already come.*

*"Stomach" refers to a rich capitalist; "nightsoil fly" to a prostitute; "night heron" to a rich woman; "slippery moss" to an elusive person; "crow" to a policeman; "crow without a nightstick" to a priest or nun.

(They look offstage and interact, excited, as they see someone.)

BEGGAR: Let's see what we can squeeze out of her.
LEPER *(looking at the nun):* I think I've seen this skirt before.
BEGGAR: That's all right. Let's squeeze her.
LEPER: And that skirt is not a skirt who can dip its hands in the money bags.
BEGGAR: How do you know that?
LEPER: Oh, I know some things.
BEGGAR: Well, let's get on with it.
LEPER: Let it go.
BEGGAR: I say squeeze it.
LEPER: Ah, come on, let it go.
BEGGAR: Let's get it.
LEPER: Let it go.
BEGGAR: I say let's hit her.
LEPER: And I say let it go.
BEGGAR *(getting mad):* Oh, shit. Lets get it. Get it . . . get it . . . *(advances slowly as he speaks).*
LEPER *(following him):* You son-of-a-bitch *(slaps the beggar's cheek).*

*(*BEGGAR *comes to sudden halt. The* NUN *appears on the stage, walking briskly. The spiteful* BEGGAR *stretches out his leg and trips the* NUN, *who stumbles. The* BEGGAR *cries out as if his foot were hurt).*

BEGGAR: Ooh, ow. Ouch. Oh, my foot, my foot . . . it's broken, my poor foot, ouch, ouch, ouch, oh, my foot. You'd better pay for this. Oh . . . Oh . . . ouch!
NUN *(upset)*: Oh, what did I do to you? I'm so sorry. I'm really very sorry. I was in such a hurry. Have I hurt you badly?
LEPER: Never mind him. Now why don't you just run along? *(gestures to this effect)*

NUN: No. Let me see. It must be treated if it's hurt. Let me . . .

BEGGAR: Why do you want to see *my* foot? Just give me money and you can go.

LEPER: Please, never mind him. You're busy. Why don't you just run along about your business. Take no notice of him.

BEGGAR: What do you mean, never mind. . . . Damn it! This isn't your foot. This is *my* foot.

NUN *(still concerned)*: Do you hurt very much? What can I do?

LEPER: There's nothing wrong with him. Don't worry about him.

NUN: But it's my fault. Besides being hurt he doesn't look very well and it's so cold . . .

BEGGAR *(to the leper)*: Why do you have to keep butting in? *(to the nun)*: It wouldn't be right for me to let you off scot-free when you've hurt me so badly, but I don't want to be unjust, so, leave me some money to take care of it and then you can leave.

LEPER: You . . .

NUN: But what am I to do? I don't have any money with me.

BEGGAR *(incredulously)*: Are you trying to tell me that you don't even have a cent with you?

LEPER *(sternly)*: Hey, you! Can't you shut up? *(to nun)*: Sister, why don't you just leave now.

NUN: I don't know what to say. I'm so sorry. I'll be back to see you in a little while. I'm in a hurry now, so please excuse me. I am really sorry.

(Makes a bow and then turns around and leaves, stopping to pray. The LEPER *looks at her with delight, but the* BEGGAR *stares open-mouthed.)*

NUN *(praying)*: Oh, Lord, please look after them. Please extend your vast compassion and free them from cold, hunger, and contempt. Oh, Lord, please listen to my earnest prayer. Lord, give me courage. Give me courage so I can sacrifice this body of mine at any time in the battlefield for these brothers and others like them, hungry and clad only in rags. Give me courage to overcome any oppressive power and all temptations. Oh, Lord, please listen to me *(for a time prays inaudibly)*. Amen.

(The NUN *makes the sign of the cross. The* LEPER *crosses himself, hiding the gesture. But the* BEGGAR *sees it. The* NUN *turns to look back at them, then leaves the stage.)*

BEGGAR *(with a sarcastic laugh)*: What the hell is this? You make me laugh. You really make me laugh.

LEPER *(bashful)*: I'm sorry.

BEGGAR: Are you some damn Christian? Since when are you one of them?

LEPER: Don't say such crazy things. What makes you think I'm a Christian?

BEGGAR: Then why do you do this? *(mimics crossing himself)*

LEPER: I don't know why. I just copied her, did what she did. That's all. Anyway, I did it. So what?

BEGGAR: But what the hell for?

LEPER: I don't know. It just seemed right.

BEGGAR: Why the hell was it right?

LEPER: It looked good . . . moreover . . .

BEGGAR *(waits. Getting no response, prompts)*: Moreover . . . ?

LEPER: Moreover, *that* particular skirt *is* different.

BEGGAR: What's so different about her?

LEPER: I've seen her several times before.

BEGGAR: Where?

LEPER: In the nightsoil fly part of town.

BEGGAR: Ah.

LEPER: She gets all the nightsoil flies together. She reads books to them, tells them stories, and teaches them to write. She even treats their children when they are sick. They all like her.

BEGGAR: There you go . . . making me laugh again.

LEPER: What's so funny?

BEGGAR: What use do *they* have for books and writing? All they have to know is how to move their ass.

LEPER: It's good to know how to write. They're human beings too. You're shit. I'm shit. And we, they all get dumped on, but we're human. Why shouldn't they learn how to write?

BEGGAR: And that's why you think Christians are good?

LEPER: I'm not saying that all Christians are good, but I like her kind of Christian; she's different.

BEGGAR: You're out of your mind, Christians are all the same. They're all crooks. Can't you see that? I was raised in an orphanage and the Christians there were the biggest thieves of all. They worked your ass off and then only fed you thin cornsoup, because they'd robbed the funds. I've had my fill of Christians. I don't want to hear about them.

LEPER: I know. I know what you mean. I was in a leper colony run by Christians. But now and then a decent one turns up.

BEGGAR: Damn it. Have you ever seen a virgin among the nightsoil flies? Crabs and crayfish all come from the same family. These Christians are all thieves.

LEPER: You don't understand it yet. There are some like that skirt who came by. She doesn't try to cheat people. And she doesn't try to smart-talk her way into heaven. She really understands how things are, what it's like to be a have-not.

BEGGAR: She's different, my ass. Sh . . . quiet *(signals to leper; they look off stage.)*

LEPER: Is it a stomach?

BEGGAR: No.

LEPER: Is it a leech?

BEGGAR: No.
LEPER: Is it a nightsoil fly?
BEGGAR: No, it is not a whore.
LEPER: Is it a tax collector?
BEGGAR: No.
LEPER: Is it a white pony?
BEGGAR: No.
LEPER: Is it slippery moss?
BEGGAR: Yeah, it's slippery moss.
LEPER: What kind of slippery moss?
BEGGAR: Crow slippery moss.
LEPER *(in surprise):* Nightsoil slippery moss?
BEGGAR: No, a crow without a club.
LEPER *(looking at the sky):* It's dawn *(pause).* Is it a skirt again?
BEGGAR: No, it's pants this time. Let's see if this Christian is different?
LEPER: I've never seen *this* set of pants before.

(The PRIEST *appears on the stage on the way to somewhere.)*

BEGGAR *(to leper):* Let's go.
LEPER: Let's go.
BEGGAR and LEPER *(They both sing a Gaksori song):*
Hey, siku, siku, we are entering but it's difficult.

(They go into shamanistic trance state through singing).

Gaksori came here again last year.
Lived another cruel year to come again. P'umbap pa P'umbap pa.
Father, I'm so glad to see you.
Father, I am glad that I like you.
My pants don't suit the season.
Your pants are lined with cotton.
P'umbap pa. P'umbap pa.

Our wretched bellies are empty.
Our pockets are empty too.
We shiver all over our miserable bodies.
Why must we go on living?
P'umbap pa P'umbap Eeh Siku, siku P'umbap pa.

*(*BEGGAR *sings with* LEPER *but again mocks the actions described in song.)*

Hold up letter one and look at it.
It's a beggar's fate to have no job.
Hold up letter two and look at it.
Ah, the world stands on its head.
Hold up letter three and look at it.
Lots of bustle in the Samilla Building.
Hold up letter four and look at it.
Evil gets more rewards than good.
Hold up letter five and look at it.
Chaos—caused by all Five Bandits.
Hold up letter six and look at it.
Crowds make a festival of an animal-slaughtering.
Hold up letter seven and look at it.
Stir lacquer so fast and the stick catches fire.
Hold up letter eight and look at it.
Lament about sad fate that comes unsummoned.
Hold up letter nine and look at it.
For the world to be saved the Savior *must* come.
Hold up letter ten and look at it.
You're to give me some ten-*won* bills.
P'umbap pa, P'umbap pa
Eh hu siku siku, we are entering but it's difficult.

(While the BEGGAR *and* LEPER *sing the Gaksori song, the* PRIEST *tries to get away. The* BEGGAR *and* LEPER *try to stop him repeating their attempts but making a dance of them.)*

LEPER and BEGGAR: Give us something, please.

PRIEST: I'm in a hurry *(tries to avoid them).*

BEGGAR *(standing in the priest's way):* Give us alms, please.

PRIEST *(trying to avoid him):* I don't have time.

LEPER *(stands in the priest's way):* We're cold!

PRIEST *(avoiding them and holding his nose):* Oh, what a smell! I have a long way to go yet.

BEGGAR *(stands in the priest's way):* Everyone treats us badly. Nothing but contempt, oppression, and scorn from everyone.

PRIEST *(trying to avoid them):* I said I'm in a hurry.

LEPER *(stands in priest's way):* Nothing to depend on in this whole world. No home, not even a temple to sleep in, . . . no place to come to, no place to go to . . .

PRIEST *(still trying to avoid them, still holding his nose):* Oh, what an odor, what a smell! . . . Can't you get out of the way?

BEGGAR *(blocking him):* A life without life. That is a pitiful life.

PRIEST: I'm meeting someone.

LEPER *(standing in the priest's way):* You shouldn't treat a beggar like that.

PRIEST *(trying to avoid holding his nose):* Oh, that smell. Why are you bothering me?

BEGGAR: If you want to go to heaven, don't treat the beggar this way.

PRIEST: Why do you bother me? What makes you think that a priest has money? It would be a different matter if there were only one or two of you in the world. But there you are, day in day out, hordes of you, blocking up the streets. Even a millionaire couldn't cope with your constant demands. *(Puts hand in his pocket and begins to fumble around.* BEGGAR *and* LEPER *exchange winks.)* You're healthy but you would't dream of working for a living, not you. All you think about is begging, bothering your neighbor. First, "give me a penny," then, "give me two pennies." It's a sin.

It's a sin. You're healthy. There's no reason why you shouldn't work. No work, then no food. Just because I give you money sometimes doesn't mean I am an easy touch. What do you think I am? A rice cake handed to you at a marriage festival or some other ceremonious occasion in someone's house? A sweet to be gobbled up by you? You must think I am the Bank of Korea.

(The BEGGAR *and the* LEPER *exchange looks.)*

PRIEST: You really think I'm a soft touch, don't you? *(offers them some small coins)*

BEGGAR *(faking dignity):* We can't accept small sums.

PRIEST: What?

LEPER: We can do without your pennies.

PRIEST: What?

BEGGAR: And why the big harangue for a single penny?

PRIEST: What?

LEPER: Why do you hold your nose? You think a leper is not a human being?

PRIEST: I'm in a hurry *(quickly gets out of their way and leaves the stage very hurriedly without looking back).*

BEGGAR: Now, do you see what I mean?

LEPER: Dawn's come.

BEGGAR: So? Did day break?

LEPER: Well, the sun rose.

BEGGAR: Do you still like Christians?

LEPER: It depends. It depends on the Christian.

BEGGAR: Hey, you need to douse your head in cold water to clear it, even if you are shivering. Does Jesus feed you?

LEPER: There's a difference between Jesus and Christians.

BEGGAR: What difference?

LEPER: I don't know. I'm not sure. But there is a difference.

BEGGAR: How are they different?

LEPER: If I knew that I wouldn't be sitting here shivering to death with a fool like you. I don't really know, . . . but somehow I feel there is a difference.

BEGGAR: You feel?

LEPER: Yeah, I feel it. Jesus is okay, but the Christians sold him out. Maybe that's how it was.

BEGGAR: You've got to be nuts. What's the matter with you? Don't you get it even now? Ha! You must have been born yesterday. There can't be anyone else in this world who doesn't know that the Christians sold out Jesus.

LEPER *(mocking):* You're really a smart guy, aren't you. Now, I am going to ask a really smart guy a "divine" question. Your honor, just who is this Jesus who was sold out by the Christians?

BEGGAR: You think I can't answer that simple question, don't you?

LEPER: Yeah, that's why I'm asking it.

BEGGAR: Hah. Your stomach has been empty for so long your head's become empty as well. Jesus is the one standing over there with open hands *(points to statue)*. Now do you understand? See, that guy over there *(points to the Jesus statue again)*.

LEPER: That's Jesus! You talk like the biggest fool in a village of fools. You dumbhead, that's only cement. That's not Jesus. That's cement made to look like Jesus. That's not what I mean. I mean the *real Jesus.*

BEGGAR: Real Jesus. Who is the real Jesus?

LEPER: Do you know or don't you?

BEGGAR: Hell, if I knew would I be squatting here with you, living like this in this shit. Do you have to act as stupid as a leftover cowhead?

LEPER: Shut up *(hand on chest)*. This honorable guy is doing research on the whole question. This honorable guy's rank is different from that outcast birth of yours. Do you hear? Hey you!

BEGGAR: Shush . . . be silent. Somebody's coming.

LEPER: Is it a stomach?

BEGGAR: It's a stomach.

LEPER: What kind of a stomach?

BEGGAR: A company president's stomach *(motioning with his hands to indicate a sizable paunch).*

LEPER: How big?

BEGGAR: As big as Namsan Hill.

LEPER: But is it full?

BEGGAR: Really full.

LEPER: With nightsoil?

BEGGAR: With gold dust.

LEPER: Is that for real?

BEGGAR: It's real.

LEPER: Great! *(begins to move)* Here goes . . .

BEGGAR: Me too.

LEPER: Watch me dance.

BEGGAR: I'll keep time with you.

*(*COMPANY PRESIDENT *appears on the stage. Arrogantly, rudely swaggering, he looks around, turning in all directions, popping his big stomach in and out. The* LEPER *stands in his way and begins to dance. With out-of-shape hands and face he twists his body in the Ogwandae leper's dance, revealing the leper's unbearable pain. Sad flute music is heard in the background.* COMPANY PRESIDENT *removes handerkerchief from his pocket and covers his nose against the odor with a great flourish. He regards the leper with a fixed look of disdain, as if he were an undesirable insect. While the dance proceeds, the* BEGGAR *cries out, high, long, and repeatedly, through his nose in a melancholy, ghastly, and movingly sad manner.)*

BEGGAR *(slyly, wheedling):* He is a leper. Why don't you give us something? Start accumulating some virtuous deeds, then you will enter heaven. He is an out-of-shape, battered, consumed leper. He is . . . a leper. Please give . . . and start accumulating some good deeds.

(As soon as the dance is over the BEGGAR *and* LEPER *dart forward then bow before the company president. Thy stand apart, put out their hands, saying in unison:)*

Why don't you start accumulating some virtuous deeds.
That way you can enter heaven.

[*I leave this space blank for you to use your own imagination and improvise this section.*—Kim Chi Ha, Autumn 1974]

(COMPANY PRESIDENT, *still covering his nose with a handkerchief, laughs.)*

BEGGAR and LEPER *(bowing again):* You could help us.
COMPANY PRESIDENT: Help you?
BEGGAR and LEPER *(in unison and bowing again):* We are hungry. We need money for food.
COMPANY PRESIDENT *(taking the handkerchief away from his nose in order to speak):* Give you money? Do you think I'm a fool? Since when do I know you well enough to give you money? I'd have to make the great effort of putting my hand in my pocket as well as spoiling this unwrinkled clean money for you, and I'd be taking the food out of my son's mouth. To even give you the loose tobacco from my cigarettes would be to rob my maid of it. What a heartless and greedy bunch you are *(crossing himself, while facing the Jesus figure).* Amen. Isn't that true Jesus?
Jesus, that gold crown on your head, it *really* suits you. It's perfect. You are truly the king of this world when you wear that crown. You are the king of kings. You are handsome, you are really handsome in that crown. Dear Jesus, never forget that your gold crown was *made* from the cash contributed by yours truly last Christmas. Furthermore, Jesus, this year be sure that no one but me gets the contracts for all the missionary church construc-

The Leper and the Company President

tion large or small *(laughs)*. Please, Jesus, help me make more money. And if you do that for me, Jesus, next Christmas I'll cast your whole body in gold. I'm not lying. Would it be right for one of your true believers to lie? No, I'm telling you the truth, Jesus. All you have to do is help me make a lot of money by constructing more churches *(laughing)*. Amen. *(He opens his mouth wide after crossing himself and turns around toward the beggar and leper. They are standing observing his actions. Then he speaks in a lewd voice.)* Hey, look at me. Are there any sexy girls around? Juicy flesh, top performers, young and pretty girls. Do you know of any? The tinier the waist and the bigger the ass the better it is. The more experience they've had the better it is. Are there any girls like that around? It's kind of nice around here, it's cheaper. I get better service for my money, and nobody knows me. If I give a girl a little tip she's even better. Why don't you arrange it for me? I'll give you a percentage *(laughing)*. Let's have some fast action.

LEPER: You really like that? No, no way. Do you think I'm a pimp? You've put the *hex* on me.

COMPANY PRESIDENT: The hex?

LEPER: That's right, hex, bad luck. But I won't do it. And now what are you going to do to me?

COMPANY PRESIDENT *(stepping back and holding his nose)*: And who do you think you are? Do you think that you, a leper, can talk that way to me?

LEPER: So, I've finally got through to you. . . . I'm a leper, a leper and a beggar, but I don't want to be a pimp for filth like you. Even though I'm cold and hungry, why should I be your pimp? Why should I? Does that make you mad?

BEGGAR *(stepping in to dissuade the leper)*: Stop it. For God's sake, stop it. Why can't we do as he asks? It's okay, as long as we get the money.

LEPER: What?

BEGGAR: What the hell are you making a fuss about? We're not in a position to choose between fine rice and coarse wheat. Let's just get the money so we can stuff ourselves. What the hell are you trying to be—some kind of Jesus Christ?

COMPANY PRESIDENT: Now you're talking sense. What's he trying to do—play bigshot? Daring to refuse money *(laughing)*. The leper's a damn fool.

LEPER: I won't do it. Even if it means dying, I won't do it.

BEGGAR: I will.

LEPER: I won't.

BEGGAR: Will.

LEPER: Won't.

BEGGAR: Will.

COMPANY PRESIDENT: Why don't you try sitting down and figuring it all out?

LEPER: I won't.

BEGGAR: Will.

LEPER: Won't.

BEGGAR: Will.

COMPANY PRESIDENT: The tinier the waist, the bigger the ass, the better it is. The more experienced the lady, the better it is. The younger she is, the better it is.

(They hear a sharp whistling sound. The three of them pause.)

COMPANY PRESIDENT: What's that?

BEGGAR: A crow just floated by.

LEPER: Where?

BEGGAR: Into nightsoil town.

COMPANY PRESIDENT: What do you mean, a crow?

LEPER: He means a cop, idiot.

COMPANY PRESIDENT: A cop? *(stunned, he tries to escape)*

BEGGAR: Just where do you think you're going? You've got an account to settle up. There's a tiny-waisted, big-assed lady waiting for you.

COMPANY PRESIDENT: I'm not interested. This is a terrible embarrassment. Get out of my way.

BEGGAR: There's a really young, experienced lady waiting for you.

COMPANY PRESIDENT: Listen you. Get out of my way. This could ruin me. I'll be out of business if they see my face around here.

BEGGAR: Shit! You think you can do just as you please. If you're so anxious to get out of here, you'd better pull out five-hundred *won*.

COMPANY PRESIDENT: Five hundred *won*? You say it like it's nothing! Do you know how many steps I have to walk to earn five hundred? Do you know how much talking I have to do . . . *(sound of a whistle)*. Oh, I'm in trouble, in big trouble. You've got to let me go. Five hundred *won* is ridiculous. Quit horsing around, and let me pass.

BEGGAR: Let you pass my foot! . . . No! *(whistle sounds)*

COMPANY PRESIDENT: I beg you . . . I beg you to let me go. *(He rubs his hands as if praying and begs.)*

LEPER: You piece of filth *(kicks the company president so hard in the behind that he almost falls himself but the* COMPANY PRESIDENT *recovers and begins to run.)*

COMPANY PRESIDENT *(almost crying)*: Ah, thank you, thank you. *(leaves the stage, running; the whistle sounds)*

BEGGAR *(angrily)*: You son-of-a-bitch, be a beggar the rest of your life.

LEPER: Shush. Lay low. It's a crow.

BEGGAR *(still mad, but lying down)*: I said you can be a beggar the rest of your life!

LEPER: Shut your trap!

(Policeman appears on the stage. When he sees them he cries out in a loud voice.)

POLICEMAN: Hey, you! What are you doing there? Stand up. On your feet. *(They don't move.)* What's the matter? Did you drop dead from the cold? Hey, come on now, don't you want to go to the rehabilitation shelter? Stop faking. Get up! *(Kicks them. Both the* LEPER *and the* BEGGAR *stand up, and then squat down on their haunches.)* We've got to maintain the elegance of this city. It's the law now to arrest and rehabilitate anyone found loitering or begging in the streets. Did you know that? Furthermore, anyone found hanging around this red-light zone at night is a rape, murder, or theft suspect. It's my duty to take these suspicious characters down to the station and lock them up. Did you know that or didn't you? Were you lousy bastards trying to pull off a robbery? Tell me the truth. Were you? Talk. *(He looks around in all directions and speaks in a low voice.)* Okay, hurry up. Slip me a fiver. Quick, before anyone sees us.

BEGGAR *(shrugging):* Today was a total flop.

POLICEMAN *(impatient):* Quit kidding around. I'm out of cigarettes.

LEPER: Honest, today was a zero.

POLICEMAN: You son-of-a-bitch. Quit faking before I get tough. Hurry up, I'm busy. Keep this game up and I'll arrest you. I've got a quota to fill. Hurry up. I'll settle for half your loot.

LEPER: Come on. Give us a break, just this once.

POLICEMAN: Give you a break? You mean you won't share it?

LEPER: We've not had so much as a cheap nibble today.

POLICEMAN: Son-of-a-bitch, do you think I'm a fool? *(changes his attitude suddenly)* Stand up. I'm arresting you both as robbery suspects.

BEGGAR *(standing up):* Hold on a minute. I just remembered. . . *(He whispers into the policeman's ear, pointing in the direction that the company president just went.)*

POLICEMAN *(opens his eyes wide):* A genuine belly?

BEGGAR: The real thing.

POLICEMAN: How big?

BEGGAR: Like Namsan Hill *(mimes big stomach).*
POLICEMAN: Ah! And, while looking for a woman . . . ?
BEGGAR: When he heard the whistle, he said . . .
POLICEMAN: If he's caught by a cop.
BEGGAR: He loses face.
POLICEMAN: And if he loses face?
BEGGAR: He says it would ruin his business.
POLICEMAN: And that was a genuine stomach?
BEGGAR: Right! How many times do I have to say it?

*(*POLICEMAN *leaves.)*

BEGGAR *(almost chanting):* Damn! Blast! Damn!
LEPER: Hyu.

(They plant themselves down.)

BEGGAR: Damn this world where you die from malaria disease.
LEPER: Damn this world where you give police a rope to bind criminals.
BEGGAR: Damn this world where the pressures of life kill you prematurely.
LEPER: Where criminal punishment is inflicted on dead bodies.
BEGGAR: Damn this world where you die from a bullet.
BEGGAR and LEPER *(together):* Damn! Blast! Damn!

(A PROSTITUTE *appears on the stage. She speaks to the beggar and the leper and looks around.)*

PROSTITUTE: Did the crow sink?
BEGGAR: He sank.
PROSTITUTE: The bird chickened out today because the crows were all over the place. It was a flop.

LEPER: We made nothing either.

BEGGAR: That was all your fault. *(To prostitute)* Do you have a cigarette?

PROSTITUTE: Yes, here you are. Would you like one?

BEGGAR: Yes, we had a live one today and I wanted to fix you up, but we lost him because of the crow.

PROSTITUTE: How live was he?

LEPER: Live, live, like a dog's nose. He was a genuine king-sized body odor. A bum, lower than garbage. When I meet filth like that it burns me up. All that son-of-a-bitch can see is money.

PROSTITUTE: Hell, the rich are the biggest tightwads. I hate them. They stink. They want it down to the last penny's worth. *(Takes out cigarettes and gives one to the beggar. Then she turns to the leper.)* Why don't you light up Mr. Leper, since we've all been zapped *(puffs on the cigarette)*. Did you know that our district's going to be torn down?

LEPER: I know, I know.

PROSTITUTE: What shall we do?

LEPER: You've got to fight.

PROSTITUTE: We'll fight all right, but it's no use. This time we're really in trouble. Where will we go when they tear down our homes?

LEPER: You've got to hold out until the very end.

PROSTITUTE: In the end we'll lose out. It will be torn down and that's all there is to it. I wish there was someone who understands those things who could help us. There's nothing we can do ourselves.

LEPER: What about the nun who used to teach you to read?

PROSTITUTE: That's a possibility. And she's going to be the speaker at a meeting tonight. I wonder if it's about us. Maybe she already knows about it?

LEPER: Maybe.

PROSTITUTE: And if she does, is she on our side? . . . I wish . . .

BEGGAR: Do you have any leftover cold rice in your house?

PROSTITUTE: What happened? Didn't you get even a cheap nibble?

BEGGAR: Are you kidding? My stomach feels like it's attached to my backbone!

PROSTITUTE *(clucking over him):* Tut, tut. How have you managed to survive? Let's go. I think there are some leftovers. You too, Mr. Leper. *(Goes to the leper, hugs him, and helps him stand up. She speaks to him in a concerned voice, her mouth close to his ear.)* I'll buy you some soju wine, okay? I like you Mr. Leper. *(She puts her arms around the leper's neck.)*

BEGGAR: Wow! You'll really buy us soju wine.

PROSTITUTE *(teasing):* What makes you so happy? Who said I'll buy *you* some wine?

LEPER *(smiling and giggling):* Are you sure you'll buy *me* some wine?

PROSTITUTE: Sure, sure. I don't know why, but I feel better when I see you, Mr. Leper. Let's go now. Let's go.

LEPER: Right. Let's start moving.

*(*LEPER *and* PROSTITUTE *begin to leave the stage, arms around each other.)*

BEGGAR: Oh, my God, and then a flower bloomed on a dead tree. Shit!

(Leaves the stage following the PROSTITUTE *and* LEPER*. Sound of wind on the stage, a guitar playing music of the song from Act I.)*

CURTAIN

ACT III

Curtain rises. The gold-crowned Jesus-pietà is stage left, back. The COMPANY PRESIDENT *(stomach), who is in the process of being pursued by the* POLICEMAN *has reached stage left, front. Their movement is typical of their roles; both cross stage and go off stage right. Enter* PRIEST *from stage right, who hurries across the stage and exits stage left.* COMPANY PRESIDENT *and* POLICEMAN *reappear stage right and leave stage left passing the* PRIEST, *who has entered from the stage left, always passing each other at the pietà. This chase and crossing of* PRIEST, COMPANY PRESIDENT, *and* POLICEMAN *is repeated three times. Enter* LEPER *stage right, intoxicated; recites following portion of song from Act I (with guitar music).*

There is no native earth
There is no place to rest your tired bodies
There is no place even for a grave
  In the heart of winter
  I have been abandoned
  I have been abandoned.

Endless winter
Darkness of the abyss that I cannot bear
This tragic time and tide
This endless, endless poverty
This empty, cold world
  I cannot bear it any longer.

LEPER: Now I *truly* cannot bear it *(expresses emotion physically. He conceals his face, as if he is crying, and totters as if he were dancing).* My mind is so chilled I cannot bear it. The pain of impossible hunger, loneliness. I can no longer bear this loneliness . . . this cold, cold loneliness. I have no one in this whole world. All I know is misery, contempt, and people saying, "You ugly man, you ugly, ugly man." Damn! Better you were dead, dead. *(He suppresses his sobbing by biting his lips.)* My only companion is my shadow *(talks to the shadow)*. I can see this beautiful, beautiful shadow. Hey, shadow. You're so beautiful. *(Suddenly calling out)* Where is there for me to go? Where can I go? Where ? *(He turns and looks in all directions.)*

I have no village, or home, not even a temple to sleep in. Nobody to welcome me. No man wants to call me his friend. Where shall I go? *(His eyes turn to the Jesus of the pietà.)* Jesus, Jesus *(he moves closer to the statue)*. Jesus, what could I possibly be to Jesus? Why would you even bother with someone like me? *(begins to speak sarcastically)* Once I was a believer. But it's the clean, rich, educated people who *believe* in Jesus, those who pretend sympathy but run from me holding their noses, who give you a spoonful of scraps and rags, and say they are generous, who say, "You mustn't do this. You mustn't do that," and "Don't complain about being hungry, but suffer it." Even when they beat and abuse you, torment you, they say this is necessary—if you are to enter heaven—and they call it the "will of God."

When your house gets torn down, "Stay silent, don't fight, turn the other cheek, obey the masters, the gentlemen, the police," they tell you. "Obey them, for these are the *true* believers." This is what the people who wear luxurious clothes, eat rich food, and prove their high station by displaying their wealth like to say to us. They manipulate and sweet-talk us, deny us our souls, tame us into dumb unquestioning dullheads, well-trained pups, while they enjoy their glory, their power. Isn't this true Jesus? *(sarcastic again)* Tell me if I lie. Tell me I say this because I'm stupid, because I know no better. Perhaps I *don't* know any better. Can the ignorant ever know better? Can the abandoned beggar ever know any better?

Isn't it natural for such as myself to speak such nonsense? Who is there to teach the poor differently?

Isn't it only the rich, respectable, clever people, those with power, who can be right? Are always right? Isn't it people like me who are crazy, the stupid ones? Isn't that the way it is Jesus? *(drops sarcastic tone)* How can Jesus answer me? How can a concrete statue talk? Locked up in all this cement he would not be able to talk even if he were alive. Ah, it's no use. What could there ever be between Jesus and the likes of me? *(makes sound of disgust, almost spits)* Go ahead, take all the goodies, all you rich, respectable Jesus people and make him of concrete or a mass of gold, strong as a fortress if you want, so he'll last you for a thousand years.

(He is angry now.) Sell your Jesus and take your goodies forever and ever, if you want, I don't care. It's none of my business. What could there ever be between that concrete Jesus and me? *(repeats spitting gesture)* It's no use at all *(changes mood)*. Damn this life of begging, damn it. Hyu, what shall I do? Where can I go? Cold, hungry, there is nowhere for me to go! *(shakes convulsively)* This is more than I can bear. I cannot even bear my life, to hell with this life, this bitch of a world *(begins to weep, then turns to the Jesus figure)*. Jesus, Jesus, what can I do? *(quieter now)* Teach me, please Jesus, show me what to do.

(He vomits the soju wine and throws himself down before the statue of Jesus, in his own vomit. There's an immediate sound of a sharp wind. Silence. He wipes his forehead. Silence. He wipes it again. Silence. Then he speaks) What is this? That's strange, it's water. *(He wipes his forehead and then looks up at the face of Jesus.)* No, no, they can't be tears; a concrete statue can't cry *(looks up at sky)*. And it's a starry night, it isn't raining. What can this be? Can they be tears? After all is Jesus really crying? Am I drunk or am I crazy? *(Stands on tiptoe and touches the face of Jesus, then feels the eyes.)*

A-a-ah, he *is* crying, these *are* his tears. Very strange. Can it be true? It doesn't make sense. This must be a very *different* kind of concrete. *(He examines the statue very closely and discovers the gold crown on its head.)* A-a-h, What is this? It's a crown of thorns made of gold. Can it be *real* gold? It is, it is really gold. I must look at this *(removes crown from the head of the statue and looks at it)*. Wow, if I owned this, if it were really mine, I could use it and be cured of my disease *(begins to ponder)*. I could give money to the night-soil flies to save their homes. I could buy food, I could have a wool jacket and wear insulated boots . . . *(pause)*. Oh, how good my life could be. If only I had this *(continues to look at it, now deeply moved)*. It's very beautiful. A really beautiful crown.

JESUS: Why don't you take it with you? You may have it.

LEPER *(astonished)*: Aah! *(He steps back almost dropping the gold crown.)*

JESUS: Don't be surprised. I am only Jesus. Why are you surprised? Now listen carefully to what I say.

LEPER: Jesus, you are Jesus? I must be going crazy! There's something wrong with my hearing. *(Pauses. Looks again at statue.)* Did I just hear Jesus speak?

JESUS: There is nothing wrong with your hearing. Because you are an honest and poor man you have drawn me close to you. That is why you can now hear my words.

LEPER: Oh, you are truly Jesus. *(He kneels down, crosses himself, without being aware of it, and clasps his hands, prayer-like.)*

JESUS: Come closer to me. Forget your fear and listen carefully to what I tell you. Remember these words.

LEPER *(He stands up and moves closer to Jesus, as if he cannot resist)*: Yes, Jesus. *(When he comes close to the figure, he again kneels down.)*

JESUS: I have been closed up in this stone for a long, long time, . . . entombed in this dark, lonely, suffocating prison. I have longed to talk with you, the kind and poor

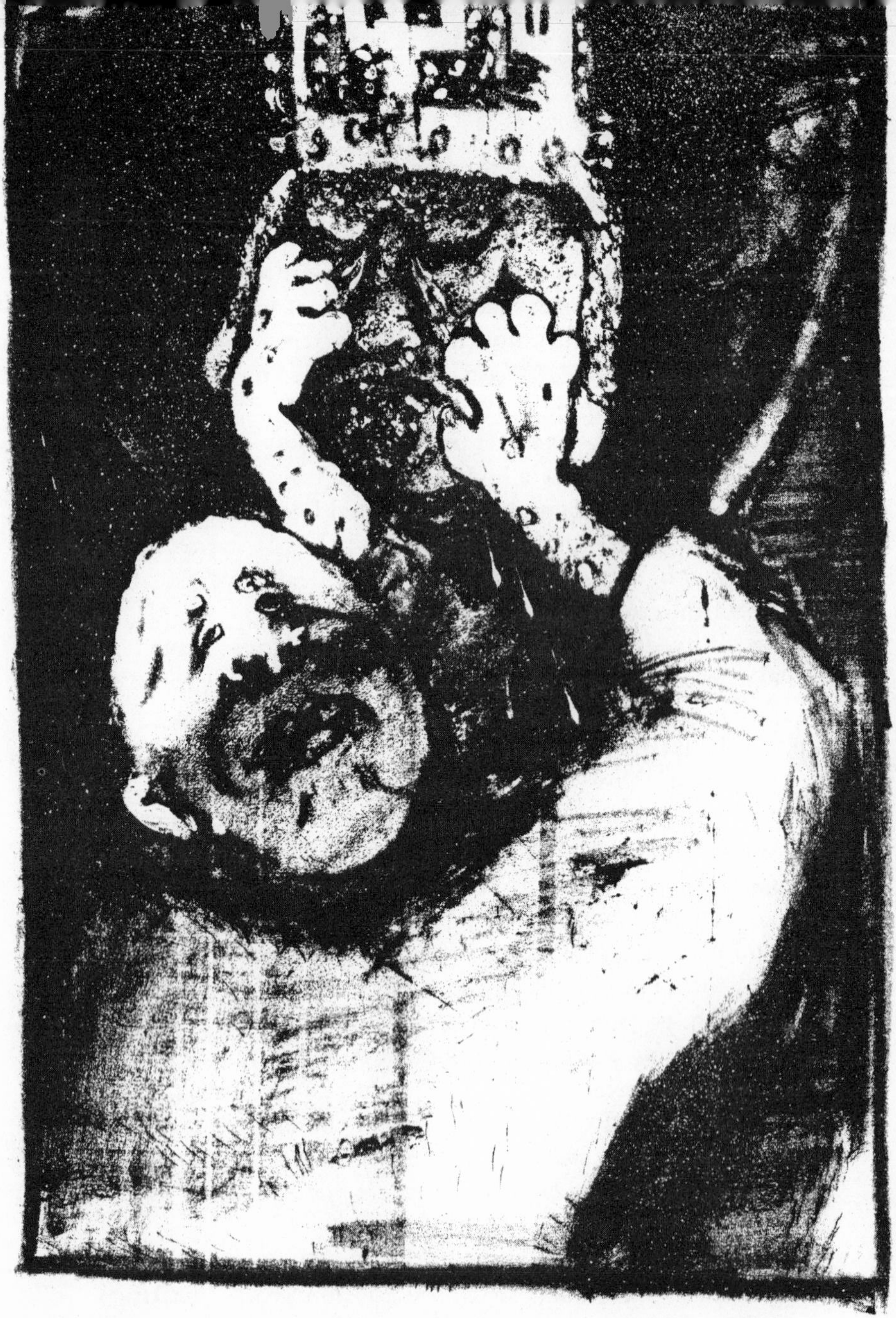

Jesus and the Leper

people like yourself, and share your sufferings. I can't begin to tell you how long I have waited for this day, . . . this day when I would be freed from my prison, this day of liberation when I would live and burn again as a flame inside you, inside the very depths of your misery. But now you have finally come. And because you have come close to me I can speak now. You are my rescuer.

LEPER: Who put you in prison? Tell me who they are.

JESUS: You know them well. They are like the Pharisees. They locked me in a shrine for their own gain. They pray using my name in a way that prevents my reaching out to poor people like yourself. In my own name, they nailed me down to the cross again. They boast about being my disciples, but they are egotistical, they cannot trust each other, they do not suffer loneliness, and they are without wisdom, like those who first crucified me. They shun the poor and hungry, ignore the cries of the suffering, and dwell only on the acquisition of material gain, wealth, power, and glory. And this stops up their ears so they do not hear my words of warning or the laments of people like you. It is for these reasons that they imprisoned me.

LEPER: What can be done to free you, Jesus, make you live again so that you can come to us?

JESUS: My power alone is not enough. People like you must help to liberate me. Those who seek only the comforts, wealth, honor, and power of this world, who wish entry to the kingdom of heaven for themselves only and ignore the poor and less fortunate, cannot give me life again. Neither can those who have never suffered loneliness, who remain silent while injustice is done and so acquiesce to it, who are without courage. It is the same with those without courage who are unwilling to resist such evildoers as dictators and other tyrants who inflict great suffering on the weak and poor. Prayer alone is not enough; it is necessary also to act. Only those, though very poor and suffering like yourself, who are generous in spirit and seek to help the poor and the wretched can give me life again. You have helped give me life again. You removed the gold crown from my head and so freed my lips to speak. People like you will be my liberators.

LEPER: Jesus, as you can see, I am helpless *(points to his crippled body).* I cannot even take care of myself. How then can I help you?

JESUS: It is for that exact reason you *can* help me. You are the *only* one who can do it. And through your deeds, and with the help of your people, I will establish the kingdom of heaven on earth for all. It is your poverty, your wisdom, your generous spirit, and, even more, your courageous resistance against injustice that makes all this possible. Come closer, come closer and liberate now my body as you freed my lips. Remove this prison of cement. It is sufficient that I keep the crown of thorns. The crown of gold is merely the insignia of those ignorant, greedy, and corrupt people who value only displays of external pomp and showy decorations. Wearing it, I was tarnished, and neither free nor able to speak until you came along. The gold is of no value to me, but can be so to you. Take it and share it with your friends.

LEPER: But if *you* have no need of it, then *I* don't have need of it either.

JESUS: That is not so. Gold wisely used has its purpose. It is only bad when people do not share it and it is monopolized by the few. So take it.

LEPER: Perhaps I will be accused of stealing it, and if I remove this cement from you, the policeman may arrest me.

JESUS: Be of good courage. Remove the cement quickly. Hurry, or I will suffocate. I already feel constricted. Hurry, so that I may overcome this feeling, and present myself before the people, refreshed and resuscitated.

LEPER: Oh, what shall I do. What shall I do? *(He looks*

alternately at the gold crown and then at Jesus almost ready to weep over his dilemma.)

JESUS: Hurry, Hurry!

(The NUN *and the* PROSTITUTE *appear on the stage.)*

NUN *(speaking to the prostitute):* Now, do exactly what I told you to do. Father is like that only because he is getting old. He will agree to help you when he hears how desperate your situation is. Please do what I say. A demonstration is the only means by which you will get some kind of compensation when they tear down your houses. And for the demonstration to be effective Father must lead it. The government will have to think twice when they see Father at the head of the demonstration. And if the newspapers support the idea of a demonstration too, he might just take the initiative. If all that were to happen, you can be sure of receiving some compensation.

PROSTITUTE: But I'm afraid. How can someone like me dare to stand and speak in front of the Father? I'm really shy. I don't think I can do that.

NUN: There you go again. You don't know what you're talking about. There is nothing wrong with you. And Father is a human being too. Although he doesn't admit it, I'm sure that in his heart, he really understands everything. Now, have courage.

PROSTITUTE: But what shall I do if he refuses me?

NUN: If that's the case, there is nothing for you to do. I will take the lead. Although I am only a nun, I will do everything I can to help you. Now, let's go.

PROSTITUTE: All right. *(She sees the leper, and turns toward him.)* What are you doing here?

JESUS: Oh, my daughters who are wise. You make me very happy. I will go with you now and join you in your suffering. *(The* NUN *and the* PROSTITUTE *kneel down, uttering sounds of adoration and surprise.)* On the day that I descend again from heaven, I will rescue my wise disciples. Be happy. Together with you, I will reform the world. In accordance with the will of my Father, I shall bring you peace and repel all injustice, all corruption, all poverty, and all sin. Today we shall go out together as one, and my body will receive the blows from the swords of those who attack us. *(Jesus speaks to the leper.)* Look, here are our friends. See how wise and courageous they are. I shall go with them, . . . so they will not be defeated. Do you understand now? Hurry! There is not much time. Remove the cement from my body. Quickly. *We must hurry.*

LEPER *(deeply moved):* I will do it Jesus.

(As he approaches Jesus, the PRIEST *comes out stage right, and the* COMPANY PRESIDENT *and the* POLICEMAN *enter from stage left. They enter simultaneously and look in astonishment.)*

PRIEST: Aah, the crown of Jesus.

COMPANY PRESIDENT: Aah, my gold crown.

POLICEMAN: Aah, the thief!

(The three of them turn on the leper. The POLICEMAN *snatches the crown from the leper, the* COMPANY PRESIDENT *snatches it from the policeman, and the* PRIEST *snatches it from the* COMPANY PRESIDENT. *In an instant, the gold crown is returned to the head of Jesus, who grows as stiff as he had been before.)*

PROSTITUTE, LEPER and NUN *(speaking simultaneously):* No! No! No!

CURTAIN, lights down and out.

DARKNESS

ACT IV

Stage is dimly lit, COMPANY PRESIDENT, POLICEMAN, STUDENT, *and* LEPER *move about looking like shadows, as if they are dizzy. All come to a halt at the sound of a drum. A spotlight picks up the* LEPER. *The* COMPANY PRESIDENT *comes to front of stage and stands waiting for a spotlight to pick him up. When he begins to speak the* LEPER *looks up, startled, in the direction of, but through, the* COMPANY PRESIDENT.

COMPANY PRESIDENT: That is correct. I've done nothing wrong. Look how hard I worked, even travelling to distant countries while others stayed home singing hymns, spending many hours figuring on an abacus, or reading Bibles. The years of living in terror of higher taxes while the rest merely feared hell *(laughs)*. The gold crown on Jesus' head *proves* that it is more right for the rich to enter the kingdom of heaven than for the poor to pass over even the threshold of a church. So, you see, I have done no wrong. The stronger the cross the better it is. The more gold in the crown the better Jesus is. I mean it.

I have built many churches and none of them ever collapsed like the Wawoo Apartments did.* In my concrete buildings only the thickest iron rods were used. There was more concrete than sand, the best *imported* Hawaiian sand. The lumber was imported all the way from Vietnam, and even my technicians came from Japan. You want me to contribute money to the church? Sure. Just see that the construction contracts come to me *(laughs and spotlight goes out on him)*.

(Still spotlighted, the LEPER *raises his hands, shocked at this speech, and tries to speak. He strains, eyes bulging, but is unable to utter a sound, and sinks back.)*

*A government apartment complex in Seoul that collapsed in April 1970 due to faulty construction. There were over one hundred fatalities.

POLICEMAN *(Turns away as if to avoid stage lights but finally turns and faces audience):* So what? What do you expect me to do about it? This is the way things are, and why should I try to be different? What's wrong with me being like this? It's all right for you. You have never had to do night-patrol duty while everyone else could sleep. You've never got soaked through doing guard duty to protect some big shot's mansion. You've never seen the bruises I got all over my body, especially my hips and legs, from students throwing rocks in demonstrations. I'm just like you. I have a stomach to fill, too, I'm also just an ordinary man, a very ordinary man, what can I do? I've got to live, too. I'm only human.

LEPER *(interrupting)*: I'm human too, I have to eat as well.

POLICEMAN: So what? What do you want me to do about it?

LEPER: You even exact bribes from me.

POLICEMAN: So who should I take them from?

LEPER: From the rich.

POLICEMAN: But you live here, too.

LEPER *(cynical, almost screaming):* Right, right, right, right!

(Spots out, lights dim. They all move and look like shadows again dancing in a ring, the LEPER *wrenching his limbs. Sound of a drum is heard and then a spotlight comes up on the* PRIEST, *who raises his hands to shield his eyes and hide his face.)*

PRIEST *(peering, with eyes straining in light):* Oh, sin, sin, sin. *(He steps forward and now speaks as if he practices memorizing a multiplication table.)* We must all pay for our sins which have spread throughout the universe. The whole world is in sin, and struggle against this is inevitable if we are to have life. We must not only face the existence of truth and goodness, but also that of evil, sin, and falsehood. So we come to the one problem, inherent in man himself, that inevitably dogs us. That is the problem of the potential for sin, both physical and ethical, in man himself. Until we have arrived at our ultimate destination we remain in sin. The more awareness and freedom that human beings have, the more they should be able to choose between good and evil. In fact, sin is contained as an eternal possibility and in a variety of forms within the universe itself. However, I firmly believe that in the end, good will triumph over evil, and order over confusion and anarchy.

LEPER *(interrupting again):* Father, then what shall I do?

PRIEST: Whose lamenting cries strike my ears?

LEPER: A leper's, a beggar, lowest of the lowly.

PRIEST: In God's name do not put yourself down like that. Do you come to do penance?

LEPER: No one accepts me. The passing dog barks at me, and even the flying bird shits on me without caring. No one treats me as a human being.

PRIEST: Now, now. Don't discard your reason that way. I give you my love as a priest. Nothing is more cowardly than a man who cannot love himself, who wishes himself some other man.

LEPER: I have not even a home.

PRIEST: The poorer one is, the closer one is to God.

LEPER: I have nothing to eat.

PRIEST: You should not expect your stomach to be full.

LEPER: I am shivering and so cold that I cannot hear your voice.

PRIEST *(kneels down and exclaims):* Oh, our universal sins. Sins of the flesh and sins of the soul. Oh, this imperfect and failing life. But in the end good will triumph over evil and order over anarchy.

LEPER: I'm cold. I'm shivering . . . Father . . . I am . . .

PRIEST: Yes, I believe that order shall triumph over chaos. I believe. I . . . I . . . *(kneels down and exclaims)* Oh, our universal sins. Sins of the clean and sins of the soul. Oh, this imperfect and failing life. But in the end good will triumph over evil and order over anarchy.

LEPER: I'm cold. I'm shivering . . . Father . . . I am . . .

PRIEST: Yes, I believe that order shall triumph over chaos. I believe. I . . .

LEPER: What? What? What?

(Again the spotlight goes out, lights down, a movement of characters, as if mixing of shadows. The LEPER *searches around the figure of the* PRIEST, *rubs his own body, then falls down. Sound of drum and spotlight comes up now on* STUDENT.*)*

STUDENT *(covers his eyes to avoid the spotlight, runs to and fro to avoid it, but it relentlessly pursues him. He gives up trying to escape, removes his hands from his face, and smiles sardonically):* It's all right. I knew that this was somehow going to happen. To tell the truth, it is not such a big deal. The way it is now . . . well, at least you can know that "inscrutable are the ways of heaven." You can call things by any name you want. "Morning becomes evening." I guess you know what to expect from me. However, ladies and gentleman, I'm not responsible for any of this.

The beggar gets poorer and the rich man gets richer. Although the beggar, the rich man, the priest, and the policeman are all citizens of the Republic of South Korea, like you and me, they are still a beggar, a rich man, a priest, and a policeman, and that is all. I'm a college student right now. Perhaps I should say I'm in a half-way state. *(He coughs to clear his throat.)* To get right down to brass tacks, what is meant by "to live"? That means to carry on life. If that's true, then what is life? Life can be seen as only a biological activity comprised of several hundred million cells. These cells consist of albumen, protein, carbohydrates, inorganic salt, and the water that man absorbs. In other words, life is neither more nor less than chemical action.

One scientist analyzed a human body and observed that it could be reduced to 357 *won* and 57 cents, and this corresponds very accurately to the exact exchange rate of one U.S. dollar to this amount. *(He coughs to clear his throat.)* Because of this, the heroes in our time are those who are not afraid of committing suicide. Strange as it is to put any effort at all into burning one dollar, you still need a match.

LEPER: I have a match.

(The STUDENT *looks bewildered.)*

LEPER: Here, I have a match.

(He walks towards the student, who avoids him and shows surprise. The LEPER *chases the student. Two spotlights move in a fast manner, crossing and recrossing as they pass each other. When the* STUDENT *is caught, he falls down and cries out.)*

STUDENT: Don't put that spotlight on me. Please, I beg you not to do that.

(Lights down slowly, not completely out. All except STUDENT *leave stage. Lights up again. Now* STUDENT *leaves and it is morning. The* LEPER *is at the foot of the Jesus statue, and cries out:*

LEPER: "I have a match."

(Voice gradually diminishes and then becomes a sobbing. He begins to squirm and this gradually evolves into the lepers' Okwangdee dance.)

LEPER: I cannot bear it. Now I *really* cannot bear it.

CURTAIN

—Translated by Chong Sun Kim and Winifred Caldwell

CHONG SUN KIM has been a member of the history faculty at the University of Rhode Island since 1965. Previously he earned a B.S. degree from Pusan Engineering College (Korea) and two advanced degrees from the University of Washington. He recently returned from Korea where he studied Shaminist religion on a Fulbright-Hays Award. He has been a U.S. citizen since 1972.

SHELLY ESTRIN KILLEN received her Bachelor's degree from Columbia University and her Master's in Art History from Tulane University. She has been Professor of Art History for eight years at the University of Rhode Island. The Coordinator for the Black Emergency Cultural Coalition for Art Program in prisons, she is also the author of *Prison Art* (Embryo Books, Scotland) and numerous articles on art in prison. Between February and May of 1977 she worked at the National Endowment for the Arts.

GEORGE KNOWLTON directs the Flats Workshop, a small storefront art workshop in Peace Dale, Rhode Island. He also teaches silkscreening to children at the Nickerson House in Olneyville, Rhode Island.

KIM CHI HA has been "adopted" as a prisoner of conscience by AMNESTY INTERNATIONAL. AI works for the release of persons imprisoned, restricted, or detained because of their political, religious, or other conscientiously held beliefs, or by reason of their ethnic origin, color, sex, or language, provided they have neither used nor advocated violence. The organization endeavors to aid and secure the release of these prisoners of conscience through investigation, "adoption," financial and legal assistance to them and their families, working to improve their conditions while imprisoned or detained, and publicizing their plight wherever desirable. There are several ways of contributing to the organization's work: (1) Join or form an Amnesty group, which is assigned three prisoners. The group then directs an insistent, continuous, and informed appeal to the relevant governments and prison officials urging a reconsideration of the case and the release of the prisoner. (2) Write letters concerning the prisoners listed in their monthly newsletter. (3) Join the Urgent Action Network, in which people agree to send one telegram a month on behalf of a political prisoner whose life is in immediate danger. (4) Send a contribution and recruit new members. For more information write AMNESTY INTERNATIONAL OF THE U.S.A., 2112 Broadway, New York, NY 10023.